STORIES FROM PALMETTO HIGH

BLIND LOVE

BY
AARON ELKIN

Beachfront

PRESS

Easton, PA 18042

FIRST BEACHFRONT PRESS EDITION, 2009

Stories from Palmetto High: Blind Love/ Aaron Elkin

ISBN 978-0-9800611-5-4

Printed in the United States of America

10 9 8 7 6 5 4 3 2 1

Prologue

About this story

BLIND LOVE is the story of four teens on a collision course to discover that true love is not a respecter of persons.

When Stephanie, one of the most popular Palmetto High School students, is involved in a near fatal car crash, a young man from outside of her usual clique helps her through the darkest hours. Under normal circumstances, Stephanie would never give Dave a second look. However, fate provides an opening for Dave to prove his worth, and for Stephanie (and Dave) to get beyond the surface. But, will this bond hold? Does rescuing the damsel in distress give the knight in shining armor the pretense to assume the damsel will welcome him into her thankful arms?

Acknowledgments

I would like to send a special thanks to my students at Palmetto High School for their input. Getting to know them helped me develop the STORIES FROM PALMETTO HIGH series. Though the characters and plots are fictional, my students' insights and real-life stories were a constant source of inspiration. I hope this book will encourage students to read more.

CHAPTER 1

Dave Lyon had his priorities right; at least according to Dave. He listed them according to importance: his future career ambitions, country and metal music, and then girls. Dave figured he would leave all of that switching back and forth with girl friends to those who had the emotional stamina for it. His fortitude was reserved for that one girl that would make him shake at the knees when he was in her presence. Although it is said that soul mates rarely exist, Dave is sure that he will beat the odds and find his.

He has a vision of this soul mate, and a list of attributes that she will have. Dave is not vocal about his list of requirements to anyone, but keeps it on his dresser next to his change jar.

His soul mate list:

1.) She will be able to talk intimately without making fun of him for his eccentric thoughts.
2.) She will accept him as he is and not demand that he smooth out his sharp edges, but she will gently help him overcome the ones she cannot live with.
3.) She will work together with him to agree to disagree on some things without a threat of reprisals or ultimatums.
4.) She will agree that nothing will come between them that cannot be overcome.

5.) She will never put anyone or anything before him except God.

His promise list:
1.) He will love her more than life itself.
2.) He will listen and not try to solve any of her problems without her asking.
3.) He will be sensitive to her occasional mood changes.
4.) He will continue to love her in spite of her mistakes.
5.) He will never put anything, or anyone, before her except God.
6.) He will vow to love her forever no matter what happens.
7.) Her needs, will always supersede his.
8.) He will never forget how much he loves and needs her.

Dave lived with his father out in the Parrish district on a twenty-five acre truck farm. His father, Tom Lyon, inherited the farm from his father who inherited it from his father, and so on. The Lyon clan has been in these parts for a long time. They pretty much keep to themselves; so not much is known about them around town except what you can find in the county records.

When Dave was ten, his mother died from breast cancer. The disease tortured her for almost two years before taking her. She never complained nor felt cheated. Dave had a hard time with it and consequently became more of an introvert.

Now, at seventeen, he acknowledges when people speak to him, but he is not what you would call a conversationalist. Friends, as friends go, are not plentiful, and he does not participate in extra curricular activities at school. Dave's grades are okay, but he doesn't care much for school. His interests are more in line with a solid working future that he can feel good about. He leads a contented way of life and tries to keep things simple. Even though he thinks, he is 5'-7" he is only 5'-5", but his muscular build and wide shoulders keeps all but the biggest guys in school from teasing him about being short. "Little Dave," as he is known to the jocks, has a saying he likes to quote when he is teased. "How big is a stick of dynamite?" And, that is pretty much all there is to Dave's school life.

Stephanie Blanco attends Palmetto High School along with Dave, and about eighteen hundred other students. Her long beautiful golden hair, and her deep blue eyes can entice any male within a mile radius. Her long legs and impeccable body make even the old janitors turn and stare. It's not that they are pervs; but that she is just so gorgeous that, a dead man would sit up and look if she passed by. Although Dave and Stephanie are both seniors, they do not exactly know each other. They have attended school together since grade school, but never communicated.

Stephanie, the most popular prep girl in the school, would not, if given the opportunity, ever talk much to a young man like Dave. It's not that she thinks he is not her type, but she is a prep and he isn't. Dave is transparent to the prep group, and that pretty much sums it up. Someone a long time ago started the prep clique at PHS, and Stephanie and her friends are doing nothing more than perpetuating its existence.

Like many high schools, cliquish groups' control how things are established. If a girl is in the prep clique, she must look cute and wear the right clothes. Well, Stephanie follows the rules on the surface, but inside, she is screaming out to tell everyone that she is suffering from not having the arrogant, self-centered nature most of them possess. She is fighting to stay sane. Whenever she goes to the mirror, she sees one person, and, as she turns to leave, she has to become another person just to survive. She knows she must first love herself before she can be happy, but knowing it and doing it are two different things. If only she could feel as good about herself as she is beautiful.

No one knows how she really is, and she has no intention of letting anyone find out. When she dates boys, she has no idea what to look for other than whether the group has accepted him. She doesn't realize that she deserves a love that will last forever, and that most, if not all of the boys that she has dated do not qualify. She dreams, like most girls, of that tall dark and handsome knight who comes to sweep her off her feet. Oh, and he obviously would be very buff too. But, so far, it is still a dream.

Jake Taylor, along with being the all time weight lifting champ, is the all-star running back for the Palmetto High School football team. Some say the steroids that he uses are the reason for his success, but most say that even without them he still would be the top athlete in the school. He stands six foot three, and weighs two hundred twenty pounds. His arms are as big around as most people's thighs, and there's a rumor that he was born with a neck.

Overall, Jake is a pretty nice guy. He knows he is the best sports star at the school, good looking, carries a high GPA, and can change a person's disposition just by how he acknowledges them.

So, it would not be unusual for him to have Stephanie at his side everywhere he goes. She looks like a cartoon character dangling from his huge arm as they prance down the school corridors. Everybody looks with envy, and that is the way Jake likes it.

Jake just happens to be the latest boy that Stephanie has hooked up with. Some rumor that the prep jocks only want to go out with Stephanie for what she can offer them on a temporary basis, but that may or may not be true. Regardless of these rumors, she is still the most popular girl in school.

CHAPTER 2

The whole story between these three students started some time ago when Jake asked Stephanie to go to the spring break party that Josh Hinkle was having out in a field near his house in Parrish.

Stephanie didn't want to upset Jake, so she decided to talk her mom into letting her go. She knew there would be a keg or two, and guys doing crazy stuff. That is what always happened at those parties. Stephanie expected nothing less.

"I want you home by twelve."

"Okay, mom. Don't wait up."

Stephanie's mom was always too busy to really sit down and talk to Stephanie. Instead, she always passed her off with quick comments and occasional mumblings that no one could understand. Except for the bonding thing that daughters and mothers are supposed to have, Stephanie did not miss having arguments with her mother like so many other girls do.

When Jake pulled up to the bonfire that was raising flames to heaven, Joe Dautry and Josh Hinkle were funneling beers, and everyone else was either dancing or rolling around in the grass making out. The tunes were coming from Jared Sims' muscle truck that had twenty-inch woofers. He pulled them out of the back, and set them up in the truck bed.

Stephanie had a bad feeling about this party. She occasionally has things come to her that are sort of like premonitions, but this time she was feeling it very strongly. She mentioned it to Jake before they got out of the BMW, but he just passed it off onto the fact that she was so far out in the country that she couldn't see any lights from houses.

The party was organized in a circle with trucks on the perimeter, and a fire in the middle. All of the trucks had their tailgates open facing the fire. A couple of them had mattresses in the back for comfort. This was typical for one of their parties, but Stephanie kept having trouble coming to grips with her bad feeling. She tried to cover it up with a couple of beers that Jake prodded her to drink.

There were a couple of typical disagreements, and one or two scuffles. As parties go this was to be expected. About eleven thirty Stephanie began bugging Jake to take her home. Despite drinking five or six beers, she still couldn't get the bad feeling out of her head. It took ten minutes of nagging to provoke Jake to leave. They made the rounds to say their goodbyes. Jake's BMW went flying out of the field on to the back road toward town leaving a cloud of debris in its wake.

Jake never seemed to talk to Stephanie like she wanted; he always talked at her, or conversed about his favorite subject: himself, or what he wanted her to do. By keeping the tunes turned up in his car, blasting heavy metal, Jake was able to avoid any meaningful conversation. In reality, Jake was missing the opportunity to really discover what was inside Stephanie—instead of what was inside her clothes.

"Slow down, Jake! You'll get us killed," Stephanie pleaded in vain.

Jake was pissed off because Stephanie wanted to leave the party. Jake was already half drunk when Stephanie began bugging him to leave. He wasn't used to anyone telling him what to do, let alone a girl whom he was not necessarily planning to keep around for anything much more than entertainment.

"Aw, be quiet. You always spoil things with your nagging. It was rude of us to leave the party so early. You know your mom will be asleep before we get home, and she will never ask you what time you got in. We should go over to my place and hang out in the guest house where no one will hear us, and mess around."

"I don't know, Jake. I think our relationship should be based on something more than sneaking around to secluded places, and messing around. Don't you think we should get to know each other a little better? I'd always hoped to meet a guy that would take me seriously…as a person, not just another good-looking girl that they all want to be with. Am I just a bimbo to you? I just thought since we are kinda serious, at least in the messing around phase, that we could hold off awhile on that and get to know each other better first."

A look of disdain showed on Jake's face. "We *do* know each other. I never said I wanted to get married right now, did I? Well, that's when you take the time to get to know someone. Right now, while we're young, we should *live it up*…not get serious, and talk about mundane things like grown ups do."

Stephanie shook her head. "You sure have it backwards, Jake. I take responsibility for being weak, allowing you to persuade me to mess around before we were committed to spending the rest of our lives together."

Jake shot an angry look at Steph. "Just chill on that subject. You're always excessively serious about our relationship. You need to chill out, and enjoy the ride."

"Jake watch out; those pigs…"

Jake had come upon a herd of wild pigs crossing the road. His BMW was not going slow enough to stop, so he tried to swerve to miss them. The impact of hitting the pigs in combination with Jake jerking the steering wheel suddenly caused him to lose control. The BMW rolled several times and ended up in the ditch.

Stephanie and Jake, were not wearing seat belts. The torque generated by the rolling threw Stephanie out of the car on one of the first rolls. She landed on the pavement. Jake remained in the car, but ended up in the back seat with a bad concussion, and a broken arm. Stephanie was knocked out by a blow to her head. She sustained road rash, multiple lacerations on her body, and a broken leg.

The smoke had cleared from the BMW, and Jake was unconscious from the pain he had endured from the impact. The BMW was somewhat hidden because of the depth of the ditch. Whatever the ditch didn't cover the underbrush did.

If it weren't for Stephanie lying in the road, no one would have thought there was a wreck. Two of the pigs they struck lay dead in the bushes along the road. Three more pigs were hit as the BMW rolled.

They survived with only a couple of cuts. Frightened and squealing, the injured hogs ran away with the herd.

CHAPTER 3

Not more than a half hour later, Dave Lyon came driving down the road heading for home. He had been out late fishing. Dave was a little tired and certainly never expected to find a girl lying in the middle of the road. He nearly ran over her.

Dazed and confused, Dave swerved the F-150 within a few feet of the girl lying in the road. He slammed the truck into reverse, and spun 180-degrees to get the headlights to shine on the middle of the road where she lay. He threw open the door and jumped out to see what he could do.

When Dave touched her shoulder, he shivered for some reason. He was only trying to roll her over to see if she was still alive, and to check out her injuries. His jaw dropped when he recognized the girl. Immediately he put his ear close to her mouth to hear if she was still breathing. Next, he checked for a pulse. He could barely make out any breathing, and could not feel a pulse in her wrist. Gently pressing his two fingers to the jugular vein in the left side of her neck, he hoped to find a pulse of any strength. The adrenaline pumping through his veins caused Dave's breathing to become erratic and labored. He clenched his fists and shook his arms in an attempt to refocus. He was petrified with fear for Stephanie.

Again, Dave placed two fingers to her neck. If there was a pulse, it was very weak. He sensed the dire urgency of the moment, and decided to act immediately in order to save her life. With very shallow breathing and a faint pulse, the risk of waiting for an ambulance would have certainly put her in danger of death. He needed to act decisively to save her life. He quickly examined her beautiful body for any other life threatening injuries. Except for a few cuts and abrasions, the broken leg was all he found.

Dave ran to the truck, flung open the passenger side door and returned to her side in seconds. Though Dave knew it wasn't a good idea to move her without proper equipment, he realized that her life depended on whether he acted responsibly or not in taking her to the hospital.

Carefully picking up her limp body, his bulging biceps curled around her, keeping her secure and safe as he carried her to the truck—placing her fragile body on the front seat. Then he closed the passenger door and ran around to the driver's side.

Just before putting the F-150 in drive, Dave's thinking caught up to him. How did Stephanie end up in the middle of the road? It was dark. With no moonlight it was a miracle that he didn't run Stephanie over. The truck headlights revealed skid marks at the edge of the road. There had been an accident. But where is the vehicle?

There could be others!

Dave leaned over, opened the glove box, and pulled out the emergency flashlight. He jumped out of the truck, and followed the skid marks to the ditch where Jake and his messed up BMW were hidden.

The passenger side door was hanging open. Dave peered in, shining the flashlight...nobody. Perhaps

Stephanie had been driving? Dave didn't notice Jake crumpled up in the back seat. Nevertheless, he proceeded to the other side of the vehicle. As he fought his way through some nasty weeds and brush, Dave's thoughts returned to the beautiful goddess in the front seat of his truck.

If he continued to mess around and look for more survivors Stephanie may not make it. Although Dave knew there would never be a chance for him to date Stephanie, he was tempted to take off with her, and leave anyone else behind. Dave's upbringing, or maybe the compassionate heart he inherited from his mother didn't let that happen.

Sure enough, he could see Jake crumpled up in the back seat. After reaching in and checking his pulse, Dave kicked and fought the door enough to make room to drag Jake out. It was obvious that Jake had been drinking from the vomit covering the front of his shirt. The stench-dried puke was almost too much to take. It was quite a struggle to get Jake out of the crashed car, and over to the truck. Two hundred twenty pounds of dead weight is more than one man should have to carry, but Dave wasn't the type to let that slow him down.

Because Stephanie was in the front seat, Dave had to drag Jake and put him into the back truck bed. From the way Dave loaded Jake into the bed of the truck, it may have seemed like there was no love lost between Dave and Jake, but Dave had no other way of taking Jake to the hospital. Dave had to drag Jake he was much larger than Dave. If Jake sustained a few more bumps and bruises from this ordeal, it was just par for the course. Once Jake was reasonably secure, Dave tore off down the road, heading for the hospital.

Along the way, he began contemplating what it would be like to have Stephanie as his girlfriend. Even with her cuts and scrapes, she was gorgeous. It wasn't the first time Dave had noticed Stephanie. He had admired her from afar, countless times, in the school hallways. Of course, he had never been this close to her.

As the F-150 sped toward the hospital Dave slowly ran his fingers through Stephanie's long silky hair, pulling it out of her face. It was soft to the touch, and her skin felt like velvet. He caressed her forehead hoping that it would make her pain all go away. Dave had never felt this close to anyone before. He wanted to be the one to make her feel better. He wanted to be the one she asked for when she needed someone. He wanted to be the one that took care of all of her needs. Maybe it was the trauma; maybe it was the touch; maybe it was the right place, and the right time, but one thing is for sure, Dave was *out there* on this one. His emotions had finally broken loose of their restraints. This girl was definitely on his radar. No more waiting for the future to arrive with a girl in tow. He had arrived at the exact time that a girl was more important than anything else.

Even at top speed it took about twenty-seven minutes to get to the hospital. Dave pulled right up to the emergency room entrance, and before anyone could appear, he had Stephanie in his arms again. The rush of the moment made Dave feel important for the first time in his life. It was as if *destiny* had been on his side. He was meant to find Stephanie and save her life. He was that knight she was waiting for; or so he hoped.

Stephanie was already on a gurney by the time Dave saw Jake being pulled from the back of his truck. Jake struggled with the attendants who were trying to get him on a gurney. You could tell he was out of it. Then again, it could have been that Jake was still sauced.

As they wheeled Jake into the emergency entrance, he leaned over and puked all over the attendant at the rear of the gurney. The smell was repulsive.

Dave jumped back into his truck and pulled around the side to park. Blood from Stephanie's injuries was still smeared on his front seat, and his clothes.

CHAPTER 4

The police soon arrived and began questioning Dave as the ER physician worked on Stephanie and Jake.

"So, what happened to these two?" the state police officer questioned.

"Well, I was coming home from fishing when I came upon Stephanie lying in the middle of the road. I swerved to miss her, and stopped nearby. When I checked her pulse and breathing I realized by the time I would have called the ambulance she might die…so I just put her in my truck, and brought her here."

The officer's expression became stern. "Do you realize that by moving her and the boy that you could be liable for any further complications due to the accident? You are not an EMT."

Dave stammered for words. "I…I wasn't too much… thinking of that. She was in such bad shape, and…and I didn't have a cell phone to call 911. I only could think of getting her to the hospital."

The officer opened a small black writing pad. "You refer to this girl as if you know her, and do you also know the boy that you brought in?"

"Ah, yeah. We all go to Palmetto High."

"Well, tell me their names, and where the wreck took place. Is there any debris in the road?"

"Stephanie Blanco is the girls name, and Jake Taylor is the guy's name. I found them out near Parrish on Erie road."

21

The officer's posture was somewhat accusatory as he pressed on with the next question. "Did you know that they were drinking?"

"I only came upon them as I was coming home from fishing; I don't know anything about what they were doing before that."

The officer's tone left Dave with little doubt that he believed Dave had been involved in the accident. "We spoke to the doctor, and he says that this Jake Taylor boy was too drunk to have been driving, and that with the injuries that the girl sustained she would not have been driving. Are you sure you didn't just go home and pick up your truck after the wreck?"

Dave was taken aback. "Are you trying to say that I was driving? I live too far from the wreck to have just strolled home to get my truck. I could have just went on and left them on the road, but I thought to stop and help. I can't believe you would even consider such a foolish thought."

"Well, it seems strange that you would be out this late fishing and just happen upon these two out there in the middle of nowhere. These things happen all the time. Friends cover for each other. If you were driving son, you'd better fess up."

Dave drew a deep breath. "Look. I was coming home from a fishing trip when I came upon the wreck. The hog they hit is still off the side of the road on the other side of the BMW that they were driving. It happened about eighteen miles out, on Erie Road. I just stopped to help. Why do you have to assume that I was with them, and do you smell alcohol on my breath? Do you want to have me take a Breathalyzer test?"

The officer seemed to back off a bit. "Okay. Let me see your driver's license. I'll document your story, and compare it to what those two in the ER have to say—if they live. We will be in contact. Make sure you don't go on vacation without us knowing, and tell your dad we want to talk to him tomorrow sometime. If you have anyone that can corroborate your fishing story make sure to give me their names."

Dave did his best not to be intimidated, knowing his answer wasn't going to be what the officer wanted to hear. "No one knew that I went, and no one saw me there. I fish out at the point where you aren't supposed to be after dark. Anyway, I think you should be more concerned about them surviving than whether my good deed should be a criminal offense."

The officer shook his head and rolled his eyes. "Now that doesn't sound like a valid alibi, but then again we will just have to see what the other two have to say."

The officer turned and walked away.

Dave was distraught. Here he thought he was doing a valiant rescue for two people that didn't even care if he was alive, and this cop thinks he was the one who was driving. Dave recognized that if either of them dies, he could be charged with vehicular manslaughter. No wonder Good Samaritans are hard to find! How could the situation be so misconstrued?

Jake was hospitalized with a concussion and a broken right arm. The doctor expected him to come through all right, and be out of the hospital in a couple of days. They wanted to keep him in for observation until his concussion subsided.

CHAPTER 5

Dave sat in the emergency waiting room contemplating what had transpired. What in the world, had he gotten into this time? His whole life had been nothing to write home about—and then this.

He couldn't leave until he knew Stephanie would be okay. It wasn't that he needed to stay; it wasn't that he was going to be able to help in any way, but he felt that if he stayed and prayed for her that he would feel like he was doing more than just being an ambulance driver.

As these thoughts raced through Dave's mind Stephanie's mother and father rushed through the emergency doors in a panic demanding to see their daughter. The nurse at the window told them there was nothing that they could do for her, and that if they wanted to, they could wait in the waiting room until she got out of the ER. Reluctantly, they gravitated to the waiting room where Dave sat in anguish. The room was otherwise empty.

Dave sat there staring past an unwatched television; Stephanie's parents sat on the other side of the room and cried quietly for a while. It was probably close to an hour before the doctor came into the waiting room with a look of despair in his caring eyes.

"Your daughter is in stable, but critical, condition. She has suffered a broken leg, and a severe concussion. She has peripheral abrasions and cuts that will mend in time. I'm concerned about concussion. We'll watch to see if she fades into a coma."

The doctor paused as if internally evaluating what he was going to say next. He sighed and then continued, "Her brain has suffered a terrible blow, and in these cases it is not uncommon for the individual to become comatose. I'm not saying that it will happen, but be advised the possibility is likely."

Stephanie's mother raised her face from her tear filled hands. "Can we stay with her?"

"Of course. She will be in room, 225, in a few minutes." Turning to point at Dave, "You might also want to thank this young man for saving her life. If he hadn't got her to the hospital when he did, we would not be discussing her recovery right now. I have to go get her ready for her room. As soon as we move her, I'll send someone in to escort you."

The doctor left the room. Stephanie's parents looked at Dave and introduced themselves.

"I'm sorry, my name is Kathy, and this is Steve. We are so thankful that you were able to help my daughter. The police told us that they were still investigating the accident, and that they needed a few days to piece it together. Do you know what happened?"

"I'm Dave Lyon. I was coming home from a fishing trip when I saw your daughter lying in the road. To make a long story short, I brought her and Jake here as fast as I could because I knew that if I waited for the ambulance it would be too late."

Stephanie's father extended his hand to shake Dave's as Mrs. Blanco spoke. "I'm so glad that you did what you did. Even though our Stephanie is still in critical condition, I know she will have a chance to survive because of your quick thinking. I'll be sure to tell her when she awakens."

Mrs. Blanco immediately began to cry after thanking Dave. The thought still lingered in her mind as to whether Stephanie would live or not.

Dave stood, and excused himself to go home. He didn't feel there could be anything more he could do here. Before he exited the door, Steve Blanco spoke up and said that he would be grateful if Dave would come visit Stephanie once in awhile, saying, "Anyone who would go as far as you did to save my only daughter's life must be a good man. It would be good for Stephanie to have someone that kind to visit her. Her mother and I are very busy people and to tell the truth we don't always spend enough time with Stephanie; but we do love her."

Dave smiled appreciatively as he walked to his truck. This had been a long night. The morning sun was slowly peeking its head above the water with a bright red glare as Dave drove slowly across the Green Bridge. The humid air made him feel even more tired. I've got to get some sleep." He said quietly to himself.

Another few days and school will be back in session. This drama will not fade in anyone's memory too soon. Getting home was a chore, but Dave managed it one more time. With sleepy eyes, he threw himself on his bed without even undressing. He wasn't too concerned whether or not he smelled like fish, and had someone else's blood all over him; he was too tired and exhausted to care.

He fell asleep dreaming of Stephanie taking him in her arms and confessing her blind love for him.

CHAPTER 6

Working at home on the farm was relaxing for Dave. He didn't have to think about relationships, school, or anything else, but when the police showed up at his house to talk to his dad, he knew it wasn't going to be a good day.

"Can I help you?"

Dave's father excused his inability to shake the officer's hand because of the grease that was on his hands. He had been changing the oil and greasing the Oliver tractor.

"Well, sir. It appears that your son was at a party a couple of nights ago out at the Hinkle place. He and a couple of kids hit a couple of pigs on the way home, and crashed the car they were driving. The car was messed up pretty bad, and so were the other two in the car; in fact, the girl in the car is in a coma, and does not show much hope of recovering. Now, I don't think your boy was drinking, but the other two tested positive enough to get a DUI citation, and their driver's license suspended. The interrogating officer did not do a Breathalyzer test on your boy that night, so we have no idea outside of what the other two can tell us whether he was drinking or not.

As it stands we can't do anything about that now, but if the girl dies we have a case of vehicular manslaughter and reckless operation of a vehicle."

"I thought you said it was an accident, and that they hit some wild pigs."

"Yes, they did hit some pigs, but from the information we collected from the scene it appeared that the driver was driving very fast when he saw the pigs, and could have missed them if he were going the speed limit. Now, I'm just out here on a courtesy call to let you know the score, and to make sure you keep your boy around in case we need to question him more."

"He told me he was out fishing that night, and that he came upon the wreck. How is it that you think he was driving, and why didn't he get hurt?"

"I'm sure it will all work out in court. Just keep him close by, and we will be in touch. The other boy that was in the wreck told us all about how he asked Dave to drive him and Stephanie Blanco home after the party. We questioned the Hinkle boy too, and he corroborated his story."

As the officer pulled out, Dave walked up to his dad to hear the score. The hurt look his father had made it clear that this wasn't going down well with him.

"Why did you lie to me about the other night?"

"I didn't, Dad. Jake must be trying to cover his tracks. Someone must have told him who brought him to the hospital. So, he probably figured to pin this wreck on me to keep from getting a DUI. He no doubt called Hinkle to back him up. I don't even talk, or associate with those guys."

"You know that Taylor gang has a lot of pull in this county. If that boy says you did it you will be hard to say otherwise without a good alibi."

"No one saw me out at the point, and I didn't stop anywhere except the hospital."

"Well, let's get this tractor started, and get those fields cleaned up."

The two of them said nothing else of the incident and went to work. Dave and his dad worked well together on the farm, but when it comes to talking, they keep it to a minimum.

Jake woke up a couple of hours after Dave got him to the hospital. They had him patched up, and resting. When Jake questioned as to how he ended up in the hospital the nurse told him the story of Dave's rescue. As he lay in his hospital bed aching from the bumps and bruises, Jake contrived the plan to frame Dave. It wasn't that he wanted to hurt Dave; he just didn't need to get stung with a DUI and possible vehicular manslaughter. If Stephanie died, he sure didn't want that on his record. It was nice of Dave to come along when he did, but Jake couldn't afford to have this incident on his record.

Jake was released from the hospital the next day. He didn't even look in on Stephanie who was currently hooked up head to foot on all kinds of machines. Her mom and dad took turns staying with her for the first few days, but when Monday came, they had to get back to work, so the vigil was over.

For the next several weeks Stephanie's parents visited less and less. Outside of dealing with occasional conferences with the doctors they felt that their time would be best spent working. It may have seemed cruel that they quit coming so much, but life had to go on.

Dave didn't hear much at school, but knew they were all gossiping about the wreck. The quick look away, and the occasional pat on the back made it evident that the whole school must think he was the criminal driver that may be responsible for Stephanie's death; if it came to that.

Jake and a couple of his big football buddies showed up at Dave's truck after school to talk to him. They were wanting to remind him of how much they appreciated Dave for making the effort to drive Jake and Stephanie home the night of the wreck. When Dave interrupted them to explain that he wasn't there, Josh Hinkle grabbed Dave and put him in a chokehold. While Dave was struggling, Jake leaned in real close to make sure Dave didn't miss a word he was about to say, and reiterated that yes he was the driver, and if he says any different that the boys would be taking him for a fishing trip out in the deep where no one ever fishes. It was a serious threat by Jake. As he spoke, Dave could see fire in his eyes, and a bead of sweat hanging from his nose. His forceful voice smelled like dip with spit emphasizing each word as his body shook vehemently. Jake began to mince his words with vulgar cursing as they rolled off his angry tongue. There was no doubt in anyone's mind that Jake was not happy.

Dave got the impression that these guys did not want to go fishing for fun, but to use him as a boat anchor. Josh dropped Dave to the ground as they departed. He was still choking from the strangle hold as he contemplated the mess he was in.

A few minutes later Dave lumbered into his truck and drove home. What was he going to do? A good deed being punished was all he could think of, and then there was the constant vision of that beautiful girl Stephanie lying on the front seat of his F-150 being rescued by a knight in shining armor. The dream didn't include a felony, or the fact that she didn't even know he was alive. It only had the white horse with the damsel in distress scenario not any of the consequences that followed it. What a mess. He was being blamed for something he didn't do, glared at during school, and threatened if he told the truth. He might face criminal charges for reckless operation of a vehicle he didn't drive, and possibly manslaughter of the girl of his dreams. What could be worse?

CHAPTER 7

By the third week of Stephanie's stay, her parents were having trouble staying at the hospital. They did love her, but they felt that being there before she woke up was more of a waste of time than it was worth, so they slowed their visitations down to Sundays after church between the morning and evening services.

Jake's cast was going to come off soon, and all the bandages were already removed. Every time he saw Dave in the hallways, he would do the "I'm watching you" sign with his two fingers pointing to his eyes, and then to Dave. The fear tactic seemed to be working so far for Jake.

The police still had the investigation open and expected to have a court date within the month. They continued to interview those who were at the party and collect evidence at the scene of the accident. Dave received his court papers in the mail, which said that he should notify the court of his lawyer's name, so a court date could be agreed upon. Written across the top of the court document was the word "Defendant." What a nightmare. All he did was stop to help?

Dave concluded, that he might as well not fight his feelings anymore. Along with all the bad dreams, that were haunting him, was the dream he continually had about Stephanie. In the dream, the circumstances always changed, but in the end, he always ended up with her in his arms. He had watched her hang on many guys at school, but never saw her stick with any of them for long.

Since no one was visiting her that often, Dave thought he could at least go to the hospital and see her. What harm could it cause her if he visited? Maybe the comfort of having someone sitting there might be helpful. Jake hadn't seen Stephanie since he left the hospital, and her parents more than likely wouldn't have a problem with him seeing her. Dave justified every thought.

Visiting hours were open until eight o'clock, so Dave was able to go see Stephanie every night for at least an hour. The ritual gave Dave a good feeling. Maybe it was just that he was close to a girl that didn't talk, or that he really had a bit of chemistry with this girl. Chemistry usually doesn't function well without both parties being involved, but then nothing else made much sense about these visits either.

One day Dave got up the nerve to start reading to Stephanie. His choice was "Pride and Prejudice," which seemed to fall in line with the emotional aspects of his heart, and since Stephanie was not able to give her opinion on which book to read, Dave felt at ease in picking a book that suited him.

About the third chapter, Dave began to feel the bond between him and Stephanie increase. Maybe it was insane, or definitely crazy, but Dave could feel an honest to goodness emotional rise when he held Stephanie's hand and read to her. He just felt that holding her hand, not tight, but gently, might help her realize that someone was there, and that the person holding her hand felt a bond that would make her feel like the fight to come back was worth it.

Dave's emotions began to scare him. Would Stephanie respond to him when and if she comes out of her coma? There were no rules to follow in this situation. Comatose people all respond differently. Dave wondered if this whole situation was just held together with infatuation or was it blind love.

CHAPTER 8

At school, things went back to normal. Stephanie's absence was lost in the shuffle of everyday school business: who is dating whom, who cheated on whom, did you get that paper handed in on time, who can I get to call me out of school that the administration will believe, and do you want to skip tomorrow morning and meet at Pop's for breakfast?

Jake, whom everyone thought was going to stay with Stephanie for life, was now talking a great deal to Autumn Brewer the youngest of the Brewer girls. Autumn is one of Stephanie's supposed friends. She didn't feel it would hurt to just talk to Jake, but everyone knows Jake is not much of a talker. He occasionally gets asked about Stephanie, but redirects the conversation as soon as it comes up. He doesn't feel that her condition was anyone's business, and that when, and if, she gets better he would deal with her then. Going to the hospital doesn't seem to be worth the effort.

"What possible good would sitting around a hospital room with a comatose girlfriend do for anybody? I can't see any good in wasting my time watching someone sleep." Jake repeated this comment anytime he was asked about when he saw Stephanie last. Maybe it was the best way he knew to cope with the accident. He knew he was responsible, and he knew it would be on his conscience if she were to die, but he didn't want to feel bad now. In his mind he needed to go on with his life. High school was a short stay, and he wanted to make the best of it.

Meanwhile Dave was making regular trips to the hospital on a daily basis. He came at random times because of his schedule, but at least he came. Occasionally he would see Stephanie's parents on the weekends. Steve and Kathy stayed with small talk, and left after spending no more than a half hour with Stephanie.

Dave had started to notice something strange on his visits with Stephanie. He noticed that when he held her hand during his visits that her heart monitor beat faster. That not only gave him hope, but also confirmed to him that human intervention during a coma can make a difference. Before he left, and when he was sure there was no one around, he would kiss Stephanie on the forehead. One Sunday after her parents left, and the room settled down, Dave, still holding Stephanie's hand, leaned over to give her his customary goodbye kiss on the forehead, but decided to kiss her on the lips. No one was around, and it was only going to be a goodbye kiss. You know, a little peck. But, when Dave's lips met Stephanie's soft lips fireworks began; at least that is the story Dave is going to stick with.

He had never felt that feeling with any other girl before. Of course, it seemed a little, or maybe a lot, strange that he was kissing a comatose girl who couldn't say, no. It wasn't like he was forcing her or taking advantage of her; he was just trying to show her some affection. Even though she was comatose, Stephanie was getting better. The doctors were optimistic with her progress. They said that sometimes it is better for the patient to stay in a coma, so that their body has more resources to heal itself. Nonetheless, everyone was hoping she would wake up soon.

The spring dance was coming up. It was to be a costume ball with all the trimmings. The student government went all out this year. The motif was "Shakespeare and Fairy Tales." Everyone had to pick a character from either a Shakespeare play, or a fairy tale. The gossip around was that Jake was going to take Autumn Brewer to the dance. The after dance party would be at an undisclosed location to be announced later.

The last ninety days of school had begun, and already the seniors were getting senioritis. Many of them were skipping at least one day a week of school. They would often meet for breakfast at Pop's, and never make it for class. Gossip circulated with a vengeance at those breakfast meetings, and if you were not there, it was not uncommon for you to be on the menu. Dave's blind love continued to build for Stephanie, and stayed in the top ten of the gossip list. He wasn't fooling anyone at school. They all knew he was in love with her.

CHAPTER 9

Stephanie's parents met with the guidance counselors, and the administration about Stephanie's schoolwork. The administration called the meeting because some of her teachers wanted to know what to give her for the third quarter grade. No one was expecting her to do anything, since she was still in the hospital, but they just wanted to know if she would be taking summer school to make up her work; that was, of course, if she was able to do so.

The reality of the situation got to Mrs. Blanco. She began to cry incessantly. The administrators reminded Mr. and Mrs. Blanco that they had no intention of upsetting them, but they needed to make arrangements for Stephanie so that she would not receive a failing grade. They wanted to make sure that she had the opportunity to finish her classes over the summer.

The Blanco name and wealth could do nothing for Stephanie now; she needed a miracle to wake her up. She was improving, but her time in the coma was getting to be longer than the doctors had expected.

Stephanie was an only child who had always wanted to have a brother to hang out with. She was girly, but loved to go camping, fishing, and many other things that boys do. When she was five years old, she hooked up with a couple of the neighbor boys, and went down to the overpass fishing one afternoon. When her mother found out, she grounded her for a week, and continued to tell her that doing those kinds of things were not lady-like.

If being lady-like was not having fun, Stephanie didn't want to have any of it. She did like having nice clothes and dressing up, but she disliked being told that some of the things she enjoyed were not lady-like enough, so therefore she was not permitted to do them. If only her mother knew the truth!

The Blanco family tree is very big, and goes way back in this area. The family money comes from its land holdings and several business enterprises. Stephanie's family came over from Ireland in 1849 during the famine, and settled near here. They built a large plantation not far from the river. After the Civil War, they began buying up parcels of land, and planting orange trees. The family continued to hand down the property over many generations, and would be someday in the hands of Stephanie since she was an only child. Although none of this meant anything to her, many of the families with boys Stephanie's age considered this a viable option. She may come as a prize catch for some, but it was clear her heart was not for sale. Her intentions were to have a soul mate that loves her for who she is and not what she has.

Jake came from a similar background as Stephanie as far as money was concerned. His clan had more money than they could spend for generations. They had interests in whiskey, land, and tomato processing. They came from a long line of investors. It had been said that not one of the Taylor gang had ever worked for a living. That was a harsh judgment brought on by those who either didn't know them first hand, or were jealous of their holdings. Nonetheless, Jake used his influence whenever he needed to. So, it might be a natural assumption that he and Stephanie would eventually marry; at least that is what was assumed.

Dave walked into Stephanie's hospital room, and pulled out "Pride and Prejudice" from her bedside drawer. He sat beside the bed in silence gazing at her face, and wondering what he was doing there. This was not his place. This was not something that a guy like him should be allowed to be a part of. This was not what Stephanie's parents, or anyone else in this area would expect. It just was not done, and was not proper. It had always been that way, and his thinking otherwise was not going to change that.

Although it seemed impossible, or insane, Dave continued on. All he was doing was visiting. No one else visited Stephanie except on the occasional weekend, but even then, those visits were sporadic. What harm could it be? The nurses liked him. The nurses thought it was sweet that he would spend his time reading to her. Who was he hurting? Many questions clouded Dave's mind when it pertained to Stephanie. He began to think of her all the time now. He imagined what it would be like if she could only see past the wealth and class to see what he was really about. He had fallen deeply in love with her. How could he explain that to her?

As he read, he continued his vigil of holding her precious hand. The comfort that accompanied that touch had never been so soothing as any feeling known to man, or was Dave getting more out of the book than he was reading? What character would he be? What character would Stephanie be? Lizzy? The answer was not too far from his fingertips.

What would happen if she would wake up, and embrace him as her one and only? What would people think if they would share true love all their lives? Could this infatuation simply be out of control? Should he cut back on his visits? The book did cause some emotional moments. Maybe that is where all these ideas are coming from. Dave decided to take a week off from seeing Stephanie to see if his infatuation was embedded to the point of true love. Could he last a week without seeing her? Could he go on with school, work, and recreation without seeing her? He needed to have assurances about his feelings.

CHAPTER 10

The phone rang at the house, and Dave's dad picked it up. Dave was in the shower cleaning up after a long Saturday of fieldwork. The nurse on the other end gave her name and phone number at the hospital, and wanted Dave to call back as soon as possible.

"Could I talk to Jenny, please?"

"Hold on sir, and I'll page her."

"This is Jenny."

"This is Dave Lyon. You called for me?"

"Yes. Since we haven't seen you lately, we were wondering what had happened. You know the nurses here have become fond of seeing you when you come up to see the Blanco girl. Well, a strange thing has happened. You see, since you have quit coming Stephanie has not been responding very well to our treatment, and we, I mean the nurses and her doctor, are wondering if you were planning on coming back to read to her, and sit with her? Her heart rate goes up along with her blood pressure and color when you visit. It seems you are connecting with her. We were expecting her to wake up any day. I know it is a bit unusual, but could you consider coming back?"

"Well, I don't know what to say. I didn't think I was helping her as much as helping myself. I feel a kinship with her, but I never thought that me being there could help her."

"I'm sure if we told her mother and father they would be over at your house right now recruiting you to come back."

"Please don't do that. I'll be back tomorrow. Just don't tell anyone about it. I don't want to make a big deal out of it."

Dave hung up the phone and slowly walked to his room in amazement. Could it be true? Was it possible that he and Stephanie had a connection: possibly some real chemistry? The rest of the night was filled with hypothetical ideas that nearly consumed him. Even during the little sleep that he got, the restlessness afforded him no return.

As soon as school was out Dave jumped in his truck and drove to the hospital as fast as he could. When he turned into the hospital parking lot Josh Hinkle was turning down Manatee Avenue. Josh saw Dave, but Dave didn't see Josh. Something was up, and Josh was going to find out what Dave was up to. Right after Josh turned north on to 41N he took the hospital exit, and came around to the parking lot where he saw Dave parking in the visitors parking area. At the help desk, Josh asked for the room number of Stephanie Blanco; knowing that the odds were that Dave was headed her way. He wanted to see if Dave was going to Stephanie's room so he could report to Jake about the visit.

Sure enough, as Josh peeked through the hinge crack of the door he could see Dave sitting beside Stephanie holding her hand, and reading a book. A smile came on Josh's face. He knew that Jake would be very happy to know that he got the dirt on Dave.

Making Jake happy was always beneficial to anyone at school. Josh made it back to the parking lot without being seen, and immediately called Jake's cell phone and reported what had happened. The two of them called a couple of the boys, and decided on a rendezvous location to meet up with Dave. Jake wasn't going to allow anybody to take advantage of his girlfriend even if he wasn't visiting her in the hospital.

The plan was for two of Jake's cronies to sit at the intersection just down past the Albertson's in Parrish, while Josh and Jake would follow Dave from the hospital. When Dave got close to the intersection Jake would call the boys on his cell phone and have them pull out and get in front of Dave. Josh and Jake would then box him in from behind. The plan was set.

As Jake sat waiting in the parking lot for Dave to come out of the hospital his anger grew. He would have gone in and drug Dave out of the hospital if it were not for Josh insisting that he stick to the plan. The humiliation was eating Jake up. It wasn't because he loved Stephanie so much, or even at all, but it was because he was a spoiled rich kid who hated it when things didn't go his way. He sat there in the truck spitting chew juice out the window while cussing Dave.

Meanwhile, Dave was having a good time reading to Stephanie. She began to respond as he read on, or so he believed. He imagined that he would see a finger move, an eyelash, and sometimes he would catch himself seeing her lips move ever so little as an enticement for him to kiss them. He was definitely in love, or so it seemed. *Blind love* might best describe what Dave held in his heart for Stephanie. He knew that Stephanie would have to feel the same way for this to be *true love*.

About eight o'clock Dave left for home. The goodbye kiss was therapeutic. It seemed to make Stephanie's heart race, her fingers electric, and her eyes soften.

Though, for the most part, Dave was a practical guy, he was carried away in the moment. He felt like he was in heaven. He was blinded by love.

CHAPTER 11

At the intersection where the boys pulled in front of Dave he came to a stop close behind them with Jake and Josh pulling up behind him to box him in. The plan had worked so far. Dave was still in a cloud of bliss when his driver's door opened. It jarred him out of his dream world, and before he could realize what had happened, Jake had him by the throat and on the ground.

"You crazy moron. Didn't I warn you about seeing my girl and sticking to the story about that night?"

"Well, Well, I only."

Jake punched Dave hard on the side of his jaw sending spit and blood flying. He was in a rage. As Dave tried to fight back, Jake continued to pound on Dave incessantly. Josh and the boys didn't need to help Jake. They stood by to watch for any approaching cars and police. It wasn't long before Dave quit fighting back, and slid into unconsciousness. Jake and the boys hurriedly got back into their vehicles and left. Dave lay bleeding, and knocked out from all the blows.

When an old man in a pickup truck came upon Dave's truck, which was stopped at the intersection, he could see that Dave was lying on the ground bleeding and not moving. The old man called the ambulance on his cell phone, and walked over to see if he could do anything for Dave.

Tom Lyon was standing at Dave's bedside in the hospital when he came to. The boy's face was swollen, and sore. He couldn't talk, but his dad could tell he didn't quite know where he was.

"Son. Don't worry. You are in the hospital. They think that you were jumped by the way it looks. When you are feeling better, you will need to talk to the sheriff about it. But for right now just try to rest."

Dave soon fell off to sleep from the painkillers they were giving him. Tom left soon thereafter. He assured the sheriff that he would call him as soon as Dave could talk. The sheriff commented that he thought it must have something to do with the party incident. Dave's dad said nothing, and just left.

Here Dave was in the same hospital as Stephanie again, and nearly in the same condition brought on by the same person. It would seem that Jake Taylor was inadvertently trying to get Dave and Stephanie together. In Dave's mind, anything was possible. Even with his brains half bashed out, and fading in and out of consciousness, Dave lay there thinking up scenarios that favor him with Stephanie.

He woke up the next morning with a big overly eager nurse trying to squeeze his arm into submission with a blood pressure cuff. It felt like his bicep was in a vise. When he looked at her, she only smiled as if she was enjoying causing him more pain than he needed. Some of the swelling had come down in his jaw, and he could move his mouth around a little bit. A liquid diet was certainly on the menu for a couple of days.

There was the taste of blood on his tongue along with grooves that were added to the inside of his mouth from the impact of his lips and teeth. He was lucky though; he wasn't missing any of his teeth. Eating would not be something he was going to be able to do for a couple of days. The nurse reminded him that he should move slowly for the next two days to get used to the broken ribs. She then proceeded to humiliate him by taking his temperature rectally. He was not happy about that.

That evening around eight-thirty, Dave woke up to the sound of someone calling his name. It was Stephanie's dad. Mr. Blanco did not look happy. His veins were sticking out of his neck and forehead, and his face looked beet red. As he closed in toward Dave he began to demand that he was never to see Stephanie again, and that he was glad that Jake had told him about what he had done to Stephanie, and that if he ever finds out that he came near his daughter again he will have him beat to a pulp.

Dave sunk back into his pillow as Mr. Blanco stomped out of the room. What more could happen? Dave's world had turned upside down in a matter of one day. He wondered why anyone wasn't interested in his side of the story. Now, from the sound of it, Jake had twisted the story a different direction. Why would Jake care if he talked to Stephanie? He never went to see her. He goes out with Autumn now, so why bother with Stephanie?

The next morning Dave woke to the clanging of breakfast trays outside his room. He got up for the first time to pee. As he slowly made his way into the bathroom, he noticed another bed in his room, but no roommate. He had one double window looking out on to the parking lot, and two imitation leather chairs in the room. The bathroom wasn't very big, and only had a shower and toilet, which was okay with Dave because he had never liked taking baths.

He had seen a few movies where a bath might not be so bad, especially if it was one of those Jacuzzi types that would be big enough for two. There would be bubbles all the way to the top of the tub with soft sponges to bathe with. Stephanie would be at one end of the tub and he at the other. That image reminded him that he surely had something knocked loose in his head.

Jake must have beaten him pretty good because he was peeing blood. Dave figured a couple of days should slow that down. Bruises all over, swollen jaw, black right eye, three broken ribs that only hurt when he breathed deep, and a sore back seemed to be all that needed mending. It probably could have been worse if Jake had let the other guys have a few hits.

As far as anything positive that Dave could think of, Jenny, one of the nurses he knew, came in, and told him that Stephanie was only down the hall from him. He wasn't aware that he was in room 192, just down the hall from Stephanie's room, 216. Maybe tonight he could sneak down to pay her a visit. He figured, what the heck, what more could they do to him?

About 9:10 pm after visiting hours were over, Dave slipped on out of bed, and began a slow walk down the hall. He was excited, but his body wasn't.

He ached all over, and his mouth felt like it was twice the size it was suppose to be. The nurses at the nurses' station were busy working on their paperwork as he shuffled by. It seems nurses are always busy doing some kind of paperwork or the other.

Like Dave, Stephanie didn't have a roommate, so he wouldn't have to worry about disturbing anyone else in the room. He made sure to slowly open the door in such a way that it would conceal his entry. Not that he was trying to be sneaky, and not that he was doing anything sinister, or vulgar, but just to give himself a little peace of mind. He was just being cautious, and was hoping nothing else would sneak up and bite him in the behind. From Jake and his goons to Stephanie's dad, he had a right to feel uncomfortable when it pertained to Stephanie.

It doesn't take too much to make a man feel uncomfortable after a couple of beatings and some death threats. Dave knew that he could hold his own, but when taken by surprise, outnumbered more than two to one, not to mentioned framed for something he did not do, it made him second guess his intentions and motivations. Nonetheless, like a lamb going to the slaughter, he continued his quest for Stephanie.

CHAPTER 12

The chair he had sat in, those many times that he had come to read to Stephanie, was still near her bed. He quietly moved it over close to her side. Tonight would not be a good time to read to her. Drawing any attention was not what he wanted. He just wanted to see the girl he loved. Yes, he had decided that it was not infatuation, but true love that may be a little one sided. He was sure if Stephanie could talk, that she would agree with his assumption. So, as long as she can't say for herself he would assume that his side of the love story would be the one to believe.

He could feel that deep yearning inside that only comes from an intimate desire to spend time with someone. He knew it was love because it was not based on anything but chemistry. Yes, maybe there was no reciprocation yet, but he knew that this feeling was not one sided. He knew that when he either held her hand or kissed her goodbye, that he felt something, and so did she. Her heart rate increased when he held her hand and when he kissed her. It wasn't fear on her part; he knew it was chemistry! Maybe it was true love, or maybe it was blind love, but love it was!

A daydream came over Dave as he mused about their impending relationship. He would be walking the halls of school with his head held high and Stephanie hanging from his muscular arm. Muscle definition is important when you walk the halls with a girl on your arm. He could see all of the "*wish they were him*" guys staring at the two as they strolled in slow motion nodding here and there, as one with royalty might nod to their countrymen.

Dave's world was beginning to make sense to him. Even though most people would think otherwise about what he should do, he became focused on his relationship with Stephanie. He considered the fact that when, and if, she awoke someday soon, that she may not be instantly acceptable to his innuendos and affection, but that she would somehow come to the realization that he was her one and only in short order; at least that is the story he was going to believe.

He began to get tired, so he laid his head on her bed with her hand underneath his sore jaw. His head lay gently against her hip as sleep began to take hold. His jaw didn't seem to hurt as much now; maybe it was the painkillers, or maybe it was Stephanie's touch. He does believe that women have a healing touch. Her heart monitor could be heard in the quiet room beeping to the rhythm of her heart, which had stepped up a few beats since Dave arrived. At least this night he would feel like a prince coming to the aid of his damsel in distress. Even though he has been imperiled by his violent foes he trudges on to save his one and only. Love can sure skew a man's mind, but in this case, it is probably the painkillers that are giving him his vivid imagination.

Commotion in the hallway outside was what woke him up. Dave was sure that the night nurses would have missed him in his room, but they hadn't. When he peeked his head out the door there was only a janitor mopping the floor. Dave hurriedly departed Stephanie's room, and made it back to his own bed before anyone besides the janitor could see him, and he didn't really see him come out of her room; just saw him outside in the hall. His covert stealth had paid off. It seems he will live another day without a threat or beating over the love of his life. Love can blind even the most practical person.

CHAPTER 13

"So, tell me son; what is your story this time? "

The tall sheriff's deputy stood beside Dave's bed with a questioning look of disbelief to whatever Dave would say. Dave felt that anything he would say would not be taken as truth, but he made the effort anyway.

"Jake Taylor and his boys jumped me at a light, and beat me up. I think it may have been because I was coming here to visit Stephanie Blanco. Jake was real mad, and he didn't give me any time to explain. He just pulled me out of the truck and started beating me up."

"Do you have anyone to corroborate you statement?"

"Well, I don't remember anyone being at the stop at the time, but I wasn't really paying much attention."

"So, it is your word against the Taylor boy's word. Is that your statement?"

"I know you don't believe me. You only believe what you want. Just because I am saying that Jake was the one who beat me up doesn't convince you that he did it. You guys are always looking the other way when one of the Taylor clan does something just because they are rich."

"Now, that is not the way to help your cause. Accusing a sheriff of doing such a thing might be looked at as slander. You should probably keep that statement to yourself before it gets you into trouble.

You are already in trouble for the accident. There is no use in you accusing Jake of something you can't prove. I'll write out the report if you want to press charges, but I can tell you that any judge in this county will look at it and laugh. One person's word against another will not fly in this town. So, if you want me to fill out the report you think about it, and call me at this number."

The deputy handed Dave his card, and gave him one of those looks that Dave interpreted as one that would irritate the deputy if he called and expected him fill out all that paperwork, and then have the case thrown out of court.

Again, the plot thickened against Dave. Is it a conspiracy to ruin his life? Was it planned out in a precise way as to make it impossible for him to surface without suffering life, limb, and the pursuit of happiness? Why him? Why was Dave chosen to suffer all of this? Didn't all this begin from a compassionate gesture to save two people from possible death? Does that level of kindness warrant this kind of response? What made Dave such an easy target? Was it just because he was at the wrong place at the right time? Was it because he saved two people from a bad accident who would have otherwise suffered more harm if he hadn't brought them into the hospital when he did? Was this blame and abuse just because he was not part of the prep club, or wasn't born with a silver spoon in his mouth, or on the right side of the tracks? Dave felt disillusioned about those things he couldn't seem to change, no matter which way he turned. He wasn't able or willing to accept that if he had left well enough alone he wouldn't be in this position.

At ten thirty, the doctor came in to see Dave. He had the usual white doctor coat on, a comb over, and two different colors of socks. He must have been in a hurry to get here. He studied the chart for a few minutes before he began to speak. It did look like he was interested in something, but then again it could be just a ploy to make Dave think he was an important patient.

"Your jaw will be sore for a couple of more days, your kidneys will soon stop bleeding, and your ribs will heal in time. You can go home tomorrow afternoon. I'll have you signed out; so you can have your folks pick you up then. Keep the ribs wrapped. You can take the wrap off to shower, but have someone help you wrap it back up afterwards."

The doctor wrote something on the chart, hung it at the end of Dave's bed, and left the room. All Dave could think of was that he had one more night stuck in this place, but he wasn't going to waste his time laying around his hospital bed watching TV. His mind was fixed on one thing and one thing only, Stephanie.

When the afternoon nurse came in to check his blood pressure, Dave asked if anyone was in Stephanie's room, or whether she had heard if anyone was coming in today.

"No, there isn't anyone in her room, and no one had called to say that they were coming. I think it is so nice of you to visit that poor girl, uh huh. A coma is a lonely place, and any time that a comatose person can get outside intervention all the better. I am convinced that they can hear and think in that state. They just can't get their body to respond, uh huh.

You know I have seen my share of comatose people being that I have worked here for twenty-six years. Don't you know that almost every one of those patients tell me, when they wake up, that they remember people that visited them. They tell me about how they listened to people talking in their room, and how much of a joy it was when someone talked and read to them, uh huh.

Now there were some who didn't talk, but they were the ones that either died, or didn't talk much anyway, uh huh. Now if you want to go see that girl, and read that book to her, you go right ahead. She will thank you someday."

"I appreciate your confidence. I do enjoy sitting with her. You know I was the one who brought her in after the wreck?"

"Is that so? Well then, that gives you the right to spend time with her, uh huh. You have a connection, and I might dare say you could even have some chemistry starting to work between y'all, uh huh."

"Well, I don't know about that. She has never talked to me at school, or anywhere else for that matter. I would only hope that we could be friends when she wakes up."

"If I hear of anyone coming up to see her, I'll let you know. And another thing; you are not fooling anyone here about your attachment to that poor girl. We can all see it, uh huh"

"Thank you."

Dave meandered down the hall to Stephanie's room. He had all day, and the night left to visit his dream girl. The walk to Stephanie's room was accompanied with much less pain this time. He pulled up the chair, pulled out the book, and began to read. He read until lunch came. Instead of going back to his room for lunch, the nurse brought his lunch to him in Stephanie's room. As he ate, he talked to her about the food, and pretended that she was interested. It made him feel good to converse with her. Although she didn't say anything verbally, Dave heard her side of the conversation in his own way. He didn't think it was much different than many people that have conversations in which one person is saying one thing and the other person hears something completely different. Whether Stephanie was paying attention or not didn't seem to matter to him. Dave was just happy to be there with her.

Reading was never so important to Dave in the past. He always needed a reason to read, and now was no exception. He read holding the book in his right hand, and Stephanie's delicate hand in the other. His mind occasionally interjected a visual of two people who had been married for forty years holding hands comforting one another. Every now and then, he would lift her hand and kiss it in an emotional urge that just needed to be followed. His intentions were becoming more and more clouded as the words passed. He felt that there was a spiritual meeting going on between them. Emotions raged inside of him, and he was sure it was Stephanie's soul trying to communicate to him. At times, he would stop reading and just stare at her. Dave could see her beautiful flowing hair draping over the white pillowcase along with her soft smooth lips highlighting her sleepy look, and those long gorgeous eyelashes emphasizing her high cheekbones and an overwhelming beauty that possessed her. She had no makeup on so the glow of the angel she was could flow freely from her. Obsession may have been a better word for his psychological attraction to this comatose girl.

It is not unusual for guys to obsess on someone or something that is out of their reach. The male conquest is a persistent phenomenon. Dave had never put much time or interest in girls until now. He felt that it would come in time, but he didn't expect it to start in high school. The wreck changed that for him, and now he was experiencing emotional duress ahead of time. His plan to deal with this sort of thing later was now upon him.

The nurse brought his dinner in around four thirty. She didn't even bother to look in his room to see if he had gone back. There was no doubt in their minds that something was happening between those two in room, 216. All of the nurses were pulling for Stephanie. They knew that having Dave reading and talking to her was good for her.

Dave was released the next day by noon. His dad picked him up at the outpatient entrance, and they went straight home. Talk was nonexistent between the two. Dave's thoughts were elsewhere. Dave's internal dialog was frustrating. Question after question flooded Dave's mind, followed by a seemingly endless chain of complicated and insufficient answers—that lead to more uncertainty. He wondered if this was just a case of blind love.

CHAPTER 14

Dave's life was definitely not going the way he had planned. The simple life was no longer to be. Plans he had made to get his welding career going first, before he started messing around with girls, was now out the window. He had fallen in love with a beautiful comatose girl who could not respond with anything more than an increased heartbeat. His obsession, with thoughts of her, increased daily to the point of exhaustion.

Dave had been accused of driving the car that caused her to be comatose. He had been repeatedly threatened and beat up by a guy who didn't even care enough to come see her. And to top it all off nothing had materialized in a positive direction for him at all. It was starting to look like he would have to make some corrections in his overall plan for success! The nightmare had to stop, so that reality could make sense of the complicated soap opera that his life had become.

"Dave. Wake up!"

Dave's dad woke him up from a deep sleep that he had needed for days.

"It's time to get up and get to school."

"Okay, I'm up."

Dave pulled his sorry self up out of bed, and managed to get to school thirty seconds before the bell rung. He didn't mind being almost late because it made it easier for him to avoid all the gossip that must be floating around the halls. He was sure Jake's boys had let it out that something happened to Dave, and that if anyone else messed around with Jake's interests that they would end up in the same situation.

Whatever went on in his classes didn't register because all his mind was able to do was fixate on Stephanie. He justified it as a concern for her health, although he knew that wasn't the only concern. In Mrs. Hughes, English class, he stared out the window while the rest of the class was engaged in a lively debate about why Juliet died instead of Romeo. Mrs. Hughes heard about what happened to Dave, so she let him alone.

His mind would wander off to the hospital to where Stephanie was lying totally oblivious to the world, or so they say. Dave didn't believe it for a minute that she was incapable of knowing. He didn't want all that emotion to be spent toward someone who could never reciprocate. He was an emotional wreck and he knew it. Blind love had taken his reason and cast it aside.

Two weeks went by without being beat up or hearing any more about the whole matter. Dave could not get Stephanie out of his mind no matter how hard he worked or distracted himself. If he went to see her, he took the chance of being found out, and having another visit from Jake and his football buddies. If he didn't see her, he was sure to go crazy thinking about her. The choice was not too hard to make. He had to risk seeing her even if it would only be for a few minutes. Love has its way of compromising logic and making risk seem like nothing more than an unsolved opportunity.

Dave waited until the night shift nurses came on right at eight o'clock to sneak up to Stephanie's room. He knew the nurses wouldn't mind if he came after visiting hours. They were expecting him to show up sooner or later. His infatuation was well known to them. They knew that regardless of his intentions, at this time, it was of the utmost importance that someone spend time with her. Every time Dave set his eyes on Stephanie, he went goo goo eyed. He was obsessed with her. There are times when a little obsession is good, but Dave had fallen so much in love with this comatose girl that it did not seem to be too healthy for him to continue.

After staring at her lifeless body for several minutes, he pulled up the chair he had used so many times before, and sat next to her. This time Dave sat quietly next to her bed. Time stood still for both of them. His mind clouded over with the thoughts and dreams of a man hopelessly in love. Maybe an hour, maybe two had passed before the nurse came in to check Stephanie's vitals and to see how Dave was doing. Dave had finally started reading again, but had stopped just minutes before the nurse came in. She was happy to see that he had come back to read to Stephanie. They had their usual small talk as she checked Stephanie's blood pressure and temperature. When she finished, she patted Dave on the shoulder for confirmation; and left the room.

Nearly two hours had passed, and Dave was tired, but he didn't want to leave. He wasn't sure if this would be the last time he would get to see Stephanie alone, so he wanted to stay as long as possible. His eyes slowly grew more tired, so he laid his head down on the bed to rest them. He had both hands holding Stephanie's hand, and his head on his hands. The picture looked so perfect. Sleep and dreams overtook reason as Dave floated off on his cloud.

Apparently, the nurses didn't feel the need to wake him during their rounds. About two thirty Dave was suddenly awakened. At first, he thought it was his head falling off of his hands, but realized that it was Stephanie moving her hand. He nearly jumped out of his skin. Then she moved her hand again. Dave could feel the pull of her hand in his. He jumped up and turned the night light on. When he looked back at Stephanie he saw her eyes begin to blink, and finally heard the sweet whisper of an angel, or that is what Dave thought her soft voice sounded like.

"Where am I?" she whispered.

"You are in the hospital. You have been here for awhile."

Dave immediately hit the nurse alarm. Stephanie closed her eyes for a minute, and then opened them just as the nurses came flying in the room. They checked her vitals, and monitors. The head nurse leaned over and asked Stephanie if she knew who she was, and if so could she say her name.

"Steph—an--ie Blan---co."

The nurses looked at Dave with excitement and thanked him for being there. They knew that all that attention he gave to her would sooner or later pay off. Stephanie turned her head toward Dave and said,

"Who are you, and where is Jake?"

Dave was stunned. His dream had been destroyed by those few words she spoke. How could he expect her to know who he was? She had been unconscious for the whole time since the crash. His mind was in a state of confusion. He never allowed his thoughts to consider this scenario. The only consolation to this new development was that when she would look at Dave, he knew she sensed some kinship of some kind. He was convinced something was going on. Maybe the chemistry was only in his convoluted mind. Time would tell.

CHAPTER 15

The commotion in the room started to get pretty hard to handle, so Dave leaned in and said goodbye. His lips wanted so badly to engage with hers, but he controlled the urge. Was it fear that the nurses would disapprove, or was it fear that Stephanie may not understand? Nonetheless, Dave didn't have the fortitude to give it a shot. The long gaze into her beautiful blue eyes would have to suffice. He knew if he stayed any longer, someone might find out that he was there, so he reluctantly left.

The nurses called Stephanie's parents to tell them that she was awake. They were at the hospital in no time. When they questioned the nurse as to how it happened she appeared reluctant to say. She knew they had an attitude about Dave, and his visits. It wasn't that Kathy Blanco thought he was a bad guy or anything, but she didn't want Stephanie messing around with someone with his social status. Steve Blanco definitely didn't want Dave to come near his daughter any more now than he did the last time they talked.

Another few weeks of rehab followed as Stephanie gained the strength to get around on her own. Jake finally came to see her before her last rehab session. He gave her the usual excuses, which he expected her to buy. Stephanie's experience was still fresh in her mind, and she wasn't in the mood for controversy. She nodded, and kissed Jake. All was well.

After Stephanie finished her last rehab session, she went out on the back veranda of the hospital to relax. The sun was shining, a breeze was blowing, and she finally started to feel like she was alive again. While she sat gazing at the swaying palm trees a deputy sheriff walked over to talk to her about the wreck. He began to tell her that they only needed her corroboration to finish the investigation. He told her what Jake and his boys had said, and only needed her to agree with them to make the case against Dave stick.

As she sat there listening to him speak she was dumbfounded by the lies that Jake and his cronies had told the sheriff. Her indignation began to well up inside her. She didn't know Dave much at all, but there was no reason to blame an innocent person for something he had nothing to do with. She knew what had happened. Jake was driving, and she definitely knew Dave wasn't there on the road that night. Stephanie stopped the deputy, and asked him why it sounded like they were going to charge Dave with the wreck that she was in. The deputy looked back at her and said,

"Well, if that isn't what happened then what did? I'm curious to hear what you have to say. We know that all three of you were involved somehow because Dave brought you and Jake to the hospital. He said that he wasn't involved with the crash itself, but only happened along afterwards. He claims he was coming home from a fishing trip when he came upon you in the road and Jake still in the car. Dave made the decision to bring you two in instead of waiting for the ambulance. If that isn't what happened then what did?"

"Well, Jake took me to a party out in the boonies somewhere by the Hinkle place. There was a circle of pickups having a tailgate party out in an empty field. They had a bonfire, and plenty of beer. I didn't want to stay, or even go in the first place, but Jake persuaded me to just go for a while. After we got there the usual crowd and their antics began. I pretty much had to scream at Jake to take me home. I can't lie to you officer. I did have a beer or two, and Jake, well; I think he had a couple more than I did. When we left the party Jake was not happy. He hates when I nag him in front of his friends. He says it humiliates him, and the guys call him whipped.

We went flying out of that field, and onto the road home. Jake had the music up so loud I couldn't even talk to him, even if I wanted to. We must have been going really fast because I remember screaming at him to slow down. Then all of a sudden I saw up ahead a bunch of wild hogs crossing the road. You know how they like to wander around out there at night. I remember screaming at Jake to watch out for the pigs. When I looked over at him it looked like he was in a trance. I don't think he heard me, or even saw the pigs before we must have hit them. I really don't remember if we hit any of them or not, but I'm sure something happened or else I wouldn't have spent so much time in the hospital.

And, as for Dave Lyon, I have no idea as to where he comes into the picture. I know of him from school, but that is all. I'm not sure why Jake blamed him for the accident except to avoid getting charged himself with a DUI. Although a DUI will probably not stick in court because he was not found behind the wheel, and there is nothing but my word against his that he was driving, I know he was driving, and if any of his buddies would tell the truth they would say he was driving when we left the party. Anyway, that is my story. I am not going to say Dave Lyon was involved because he wasn't. You need to talk to Jake again if you want to know why Dave is involved."

"That helps quite a bit Ms. Blanco. You know Jake's family has quite a bit of pull around this town, and if one of the Taylor's say something there are few people willing to disagree with them. I suspect that the story Dave gave us was the truth, and that indeed Jake was just trying to cover up with that story to avoid getting in trouble with his dad, and getting a DUI. I'll have a talk with him again, and see if I can get him to tell the truth. If he doesn't confess to being behind the wheel then we won't be able to prosecute him unless you press charges."

"Although I know that Jake is lying, all that I want to do is go home. I don't want to press charges, and I definitely don't want the blame to go to Dave Lyon."

"Do you know that Dave saved your life?" The officer added.

Stephanie was slowly figuring this whole thing out, but had no idea that Dave saved her life. Her parents, the nurses, doctors, nor Jake had said anything to that regard. For a moment, surprise, and then shock, came over her.

"What do you mean?"

"Well, according to Dave, he was coming home from fishing that fateful night, and almost ran over you."

"What? Almost ran over me?"

"Yeah. It was late, and dark out there. No one would have been able to see you until the last minute. You were laying in the road unconscious and bleeding. Dave swerved to miss you, and nearly wrecked himself. He got out, loaded you up into his truck, and brought you to the hospital. If he had waited until the ambulance arrived, they would have taken you to the morgue. Maybe it would have saved him all the trouble he has seen since this happened if he would only have left you two out there and went home instead. The kid is a hero in my opinion. Maybe this town is not up on his kind, but he is all right in my book."

Stephanie was dazed. The blank look on her face was doing nothing but covering up for the dismay that she felt. She was near death when this person that she would never give the time of day to, saves her life. Many thoughts ran through her mind as she headed back to her room. She had a couple more days at the hospital before she could go home. Her whole life was now ahead of her. She needed to think things through. It all seemed like a bad dream. On one hand she had to thank God for having Dave save her life, and on the other she needed to think about her future with Jake, and the whole fake life that she leads. To top it all off the night nurse that was so fond of Dave told her the whole story of how Dave spent so much time reading to her and comforting her during her coma. Enlightenment sometimes only comes along when tragedy is nearby, but blind love hides so many flaws.

CHAPTER 16

In the morning, of her last day in the hospital, Dave came into her room. Stephanie was dozing. He sat down on the chair next to her bed where he had sat so many times before. Gazing over at the beautiful girl lying before him, he allowed his mind to wonder about things. What would it have been like if he had only been born into a better family? What would have happened if he had taken Stephanie fishing that night instead of her ending up with Jake.

She stirred, and his heart jumped. He had a paper clutched in his hand, which he brought to give to her. Her eyes met his as the sleep ran from her face, and was replaced with a smile. Now that she knew the truth, she couldn't help but have a smile for the guy who had saved her life that awful night.

"Stephanie, I wrote you a poem. I know you don't know me, but I know you more than you think. Maybe we can get together sometime and talk about that night when I picked you up off the road, and all of the days and nights I spent by your side in the hospital. I know you had that talk with the deputy, and I thank you for telling the truth. Anyway, here it is."

Dave handed Stephanie the poem. The paper was folded in half. She just watched him as he walked out of the room. He allowed her no time say a word. A strong feeling filled her heart at that moment, and she realized that she and Dave had some cosmic relationship that she couldn't seem to put her finger on. She knew that all the guys in school thought she was the hottest girl on campus, but she only thought that because of all of the gossip. She never thought any of them were interested in her for anything more than a good time. After a moment of thought, Stephanie unfolded the notebook paper and started to read.

To Stephanie,

Inner Touch

You are so gorgeous that it staggers mans' imagination to beg for a nod, a wink, or any notion that they were noticed by you.

The beauty you bear is not limited to an external facade, but includes an inner congratulation that cannot be limited to mere accolades of pleasure or countenance value.

The love that it takes to quench your yearning is far beyond the touch, or intellectual barrier perceived by a customary conversation.

No one can take lightly an interlude with you whereas it might appear that progress toward recognizing the depths of your intricate being can be revealed.

One must deepen the search into the depths of your soul to divulge those innermost secrets of your heart, and the pleasures that will satisfy you.

An unconditional unabridged love will be necessary to suffice and earn your love.

Your Friend,
Dave

It was a hand written poem with deep emotions, which made the poem feel even more personal. The depth of insight that Dave used to describe her inner feelings made her realize that somehow he was able to see things in her that no guy, let alone herself, knew about her sheltered personality.

Stephanie fought back the tears racing down her cheeks, but gave up quickly. It didn't matter to her if someone saw her crying. Like nothing Stephanie had experienced in the past, the poem opened a floodgate of emotion. Very touched, she read it again and again her heart melting more each time. What was she to think of this recent information? The wreck, and then Dave's devotion to his protracted love for her during the whole ordeal seemed to be quite overwhelming. She didn't really know him. He apparently knows more about her than any guy she knows. And, he somehow gathered all of that incredible insight from not even dating her. Confusion was an understatement for the state of mind she was in. Stephanie could do little but wonder how all of this fit into the fabric of her inconsequential life. Is Dave's apparent love for her something she should pursue, or should she just chock it off to a "had to be there" experience? Those who believe in fate have a way of believing that fate will work itself out, and that when destiny calls you should act on it. All of this would be easy to cope with if Stephanie wasn't so dumbfounded by all of these recent events that she had little to nothing to do with; she had been in a coma.

*   *   *   *   *

After giving Stephanie the poem, Dave figured that he would never hear from her again. In fact, when he thought about the absurdity of it he knew he was only fooling himself. Dreams are just that way, and if you believe in them with all of your heart, it doesn't mean that they will come true. It only means that you are following a dream. At least that is the conclusion Dave came to. He was trying to protect his emotions, which gave him a way out. Love is an emotion he never thought he would have to deal seriously with this soon in his life, especially with a girl out of his league.

The deputy did go to the Taylor compound to confront Jake about what really happened the night of the wreck. Jake and his dad were out back on the veranda sipping Green tea when the butler brought the deputy to them.

"Would you like some of this wonderful Green tea deputy?" Mr. Taylor asked.

"Two sugars please."

The butler silently nodded, and went to collect his order.

"Please sit down. My son and I have been doing a little reflecting since Stephanie woke from her coma. We have also been planning Jake's future in the family business. Would you be interested in hearing what we have come up with so far?"

"Well, Mister Taylor. I'm not one to intrude in other people's plans, and well I, well I, just came by to go over some details of the night in question with Jake."

"You can say anything here deputy. No one hears beyond these walls. Anything you have to say to my son you can say here."

"Well then, I'll get right to it."

The butler came back and handed the deputy his tea. "Will that be all?" The butler asked.

"Yes. That will be all Jerome," Mr. Taylor added.

"I talked to Stephanie yesterday about what she remembers about the night the crash happened. She tells a different story than what you told us, Jake. She says that you were driving, and that you both had a few beers before you left the party.

Now, your statement was nothing like that. I just want to hear the truth. No one is pressing charges, and no one is trying to smear the Taylor name. These loose ends, need to be tidied up, you know paperwork and all. I'm having just a little bit of trouble putting it all together. We know you were not found behind the wheel of the car. In fact, it is only Dave Lyon's word that places you in the car at all. Now he has been told that he has been cleared of any wrongdoing and has said he will not press charges of slander against you and your friends. So, it is up to you to tell me what really happened that night. If you were in fact behind the wheel and drunk, I will have to charge you with a DUI."

Mr. Taylor chided in. "Now listen deputy. It seems to me that since there is no one pressing charges, and everyone has been taken care of, that is as far as insurance and such, why don't we just leave it at that. I'm sure Jake is still shaken up from the accident and does not remember who was driving that night if in fact he was even near the accident that night. The way I hear it—and that is what you might consider—is Jake may have been a little confused when he gave his statement after the wreck. He wasn't sure what his name was that night let alone what *really* happened.

I had a talk with Josh Hinkle, and found out what *really* happened. Jake was hurt when he got in the way of one of the boys trucks while they were muddin. He apparently was flagging them to start, and got accidentally hit by one of the trucks. Now that makes complete sense doesn't it? His injuries are consistent with that explanation. And, Stephanie was in the back of one of the muddin trucks, and was thrown out, so I'm not so sure she has a clue what really happened that night. It was a field party, and you remember what they were like don't you?"

The officer nodded under the spell of Mr. Taylor's powerful scrutiny of the situation.

"The way I understand it Josh Hinkle was taking them into the hospital when they came upon the pigs and crashed. Josh went for help, and was up the road a ways when Dave Lyon came on the scene. By the time Josh got back to the scene, Dave had taken Jake and Stephanie. That's how it happened from what I can find out, and I'm going to stick with that story. Do you need any more information to complete the investigation?"

"Ah, no sir. I think that will do it for this case. I thank you for the tea, and hope you get better, Jake."

"I'll see you out, sir," the butler remarked.

Even though everyone knew what happened, it all blew over in no time at all. No one at school said much. Everything went back to normal. It is amazing how soon things can be forgotten. Stephanie never heard about what Jake and his football buddies had done to Dave. She didn't come back to school right away, but made up all of her schoolwork at home with the help of a tutor. Dave's blind love continued without remorse because he was smitten.

CHAPTER 17

Dave could only hope that the last remaining month or so of school would hurry by. Being seniors, and graduating soon, has its advantages as far as never seeing many of the people you have spent the last four to twelve years with. That was what Dave was thinking. He had his welding career to pursue. If the magic, between him and Stephanie, were real then it would work out. He could not get Stephanie off his mind, and he knew there was little chance that they would hook up, so why was he so obsessed about it? After cooling off for a couple of weeks Dave was able to concentrate a little better. Although Stephanie was still foremost on his mind, he was able to concentrate on his schoolwork.

Daydreaming on his way to the truck after school one day Dave accidentally bumped into April Bianca, knocking her books to the pavement.

"Oh, God! Please forgive me. I wasn't watching what I was doing. Let me pick those up for you," Dave cringed in embarrassment. "I am so sorry. I should have been more careful." April stood there in consternation wondering whether to be mad or happy that she finally got to meet Dave. She had heard from a couple of her friends about Dave, and wanted to meet him. Dave, on the other hand may have seen April around, but did not remember seeing her before.

April began to ramble in machine gun English about herself, and how she wasn't a typical high school female. She had goals and was determined to follow through with them. She would occasionally go to parties, and confessed to only drinking on occasion. She didn't like being out of control. Not that Dave was looking for a rebound relationship from Stephanie, or that Dave was looking for a relationship, or that Dave could instantly relate to April's philosophy, and especially not because April was quite gorgeous, but as April was explaining her life to him, Dave saw a twinkle in her eye that could have been a key, an omen, a sign, a signal to him that maybe he missed it when he thought Stephanie was the one and only.

April continued machine-gunning her words, "Many of the girls tell stories of how they got drunk at such and such party, and seem to have no memory of what they had done once inebriated. I always felt that most, if not all, of the girls used getting drunk as an excuse to justify doing what they wanted to do anyway. In fact, it is quite common for girls to act as if they were drunk in order to get some guy to pay special attention to them. I have decided to not make a commitment to any guy who drinks." She was insinuating that she didn't want Dave to be one of those typical guys who go out partying and drinking the night away.

Even though she was the aggressor in this burgeoning relationship, she wanted Dave to know where she stood. April explained how she grew up in a household that both parents were drinkers. She saw first hand how it can control, and push the family into poverty and trouble. Many times, she lay awake at night wondering if her mom and dad were going to come home, and if they did were they going to wake her and her brother up with the fighting that usually followed those late night binges.

April had trouble finding any common ground with most high school boys. She always thought she would be happier with an older more mature guy. She wasn't looking for an intimate relationship based on sex; rather, April sought a relationship that would be built on old fashion trust and companionship. She figured she had plenty of time for those intimate moments once she was married. Despite the fact that few of her peers felt that way, she never let their opinions dissuade her.

Dave finally got all of her books picked up and back into her hands during her talkathon. He excused himself, went to his truck and then left. He could see April standing at the end of the walkway watching him leave. Questions about the two girls now bounced around in his mind like unruly children. It took some time for Dave to digest all that April said.

Although Stephanie smote his heart, he knew the chances of them ending up together was too much to expect. Soooo, what about April? Did love just become blind to the circumstances? Dave felt that there had been some chemistry between them. He was a little concerned about April's thoughts and rules on drinking, but overall he didn't think it would come between them if they started to go out. April was pretty, had similar goals, and liked him; what more could he want?

The next day when Dave went to his truck, April was leaning against it with a cute smile on her face, pink spaghetti strap top, short pink with brown striped skirt that showed her long beautiful legs. The three-inch heels made her a couple of inches taller than Dave, but he didn't mind. His imagination never took a break when it came to females; especially lately.

"Hey there," April remarked.

"Hey, April. Did I mess up one of your books yesterday or something? I should have been watching where I was going instead of having my head in the clouds. I have had a tough few months."

"No, no, no, David. I simply wanted to stop and say 'hi,' before you left school. I have dance class in a few minutes. I wanted to stop by to say hi. I guess I already said that, didn't I? Well, anyway…I wondered if you'd like to talk sometime. I mean, we could talk on the phone, or go to the park and sit and chat sometime. What do you think?"

Dave wasn't sure how to respond. He still had a thing for Stephanie, and probably always would. How could he justify talking with April? On the other hand April is here, and what he and Stephanie could have is still in his dreams, so the old saying of "a bird in the hand is worth two in a bush," may be the way to approach this dilemma. Anyway, Dave didn't need much persuasion in his mind to convince him that hooking up with April would be a good choice.

What the heck is wrong with talking with another girl? He wasn't looking for a girlfriend, and especially anyone that would get serious over him—

unless it was Stephanie, of course. Talking and hanging out with April wouldn't really be dating.

To complicate matters, Dave was definitely attracted to April. Who wouldn't be? There was a certain beautiful complexity to her that set her apart from the rest of the field, or maybe it was more that April was talking to him. It wasn't common for girls to come up to him and start talking let alone wanting him to call. After all, if he didn't like how it transpired, or got uncomfortable with the way things were developing, he would just cut it off like any mature young man would do. His confidence was high.

Dave took a step toward April, with his hands in his pockets. "Well, I guess so. I just don't want to get tied down right now. I want to get through school, so I can get a job in the welding trade. I don't really want to go to college. There isn't much use taking all of those classes just to find out that I'll have to do a job that requires me to use my brawn instead of my brains. There will be some math and geometry, but I don't think I'll use something like history in welding.

My dad knows someone in the Boilermakers union that might help me get hired once I am out of school. I would like to get good enough to be part of the road crew that travels all around the country, and, in fact, the world. If I get into that kind of crew, it will give me the financial ability to accomplish my dreams. Please forgive me for going on. I'm committed to my goals. Most of my friends aren't sure what they want to do beyond skateboarding, partying, and getting...well having girl friends."

"No, David. I enjoy hearing what you have to say. Somehow I knew they were right when they said you were very mature for your age. I think we can have some good chats. This whole thing came about because I was lonely for someone mature to talk to. I hope I am not being too forward. I never act this way toward guys, especially high school guys. In fact, I generally ignore any of the high school males that try to ask me out. I've been waiting to meet someone like you."

Dave agreed that talking to someone might help his loneliness. He had to reason with sanity and realize that Stephanie was not ever going to be his. There wouldn't be anything wrong with talking to April. He continued to justify to himself all of the reasons why it would be all right to talk with April, and finally gave up trying before he drove himself crazy.

Considering the pros and cons, Dave concluded that he might even be better off allowing himself to be vulnerable to the attraction he was feeling for April. Though April was not as physically mature as Stephanie, being a couple of years younger—April was available.

Love is always somewhere to be found; even if it is blind love.

CHAPTER 18

Jake and Stephanie appeared to be back at it again. You could see them a mile away strolling through the halls with their entourage. The word around campus was that Jake didn't stop going out, and it didn't seem to bother him that Stephanie couldn't come with him. Some said he always found some other "pleasant distraction" at those frivolous endeavors called parties.

Being oblivious can be a protector of emotions. Nobody dared to mention to Stephanie any of the things they heard about Jake. Either her friends were trying to protect her from more pain, or they just didn't want Jake on them with an attitude. Time went on; nothing changed.

On the other hand, it was almost a week before Dave made time to call April. He figured that if they just talked on the phone he would be more comfortable. When he talked to Stephanie during all of those hospital visits, she listened to everything he had to say, but then again she was in a coma. What was he going to talk to April about? Maybe they would talk about their similar interests if many can be found. Dave doubted that April would be interested in talking about welding, or fixing fences, working on the tractor, or replacing the water pump on his truck, but they did have a similar philosophy on life; future goals and determination to see them through.

After many days of deliberation Dave called April one night. It was after nine o'clock when he dialed her up.

"April. This is Dave Lyon. Do you remember me?"

"Of course, Dave. Why did you take so long to call me? I see you occasionally at school when you're going to your third period class. I look for you to see me, but you usually have your head down as you walk. I have been having dance class right after last period, so I haven't been able to catch you at your truck either. I know you leave as soon as last period is over, so I don't even go out to look for you."

"I'm sorry. That's just how I walk, I guess. I'll try to start watching for you from now on. I suppose that since I am naturally shy and non-confrontational that I walk with my head down to avoid looking eye to eye with anyone." Then her question caught Dave off guard. "Are you going to the spring dance? You realize it will be your last one unless you come with me until I graduate. I want to go real bad this year, and was really hoping that you would take me. I'm not trying to be to forward, but when I want something I seem to find ways of mustering the boldness to ask."

"Well...uh...I haven't given it much thought. I normally don't go to those things. It's not that I'm not sociable. I...just think those dances, well, are not for me."

The truth of the matter was that Dave *was* antisocial with people his age. He preferred older people his dad's age to hang out with. He was excited about having April ask him to go to the dance, but he was very unsure about his ability to go out with a girl on a date. It wasn't that he couldn't drive over to pick her up or take her out to eat after the dance, but it was more of the uncertainty of his antisocial personality.

"C'mon, Dave. I was hoping you would take me. I love to dance. It would be fun to go with you. I would have a good excuse to go out and buy a pretty dress. I love to dress up."

April hesitated, as if coming upon an obstacle to her train of thought. "Oh, I forgot. I never asked you if you have a girlfriend. You don't have one, do you? I mean I haven't heard around that you have one. I did hear that you went to the hospital to see Stephanie a lot, but I know you aren't *seeing* her. Is there someone I don't know about? I mean… I don't want to be to pushy if there is someone else in the picture."

Dave was stunned and hesitated for a minute before replying to April about Stephanie. "I was just checking up to see how she was doing. You know she was in a coma for a while. I brought her into the hospital after the crash, and no, I don't have a girlfriend. I really don't have the time right now. As I told you I'm concentrating on finishing school, and getting into welding."

It was evident to April that Dave had some feelings for Stephanie by the quiver in his voice. It is rare if not impossible for teenaged guys to have girls as friends unless they are batting for the other team. April knew she would have to battle with Dave's blind love of Stephanie.

"I just had to ask. I wasn't sure if there was anyone around that I haven't heard of. I don't like to interfere. Anyway, in my opinion I think Stephanie is making a mistake messing around guys like Jake. They tend to go for the girls for one thing. And, maybe that's all they want. I don't know. Maybe the girls want the same thing. People today have no regard for chivalry or abstinence."

"You don't know that Stephanie is like that. Just because she is going out with that Neanderthal, it doesn't mean that she is promiscuous or without values. For all you know she could be sharing the same philosophy as we have about life, love, and the future. Did I say love? Well I just assumed that we share the same opinion about love since we agree on so many other philosophical ideas."

"I'm sorry, David. I didn't realize you thought so highly of Stephanie. All I know is that she really missed out by not taking up with you. She could have anyone in this school, but in my opinion, she chose unwisely."

"Why would you say *that*?" Dave asked, pleasantly surprised by the compliment.

"For one, you saved her life. Second, you spent all of that time visiting her in the hospital when no one else went to see her. Yeah, I heard about it. Some of the guys who beat you up were talking about it in geometry class. Anyway, I sense that you are light years above *those* kinds of guys, and if she is to blind to see it then it is her loss."

"I'm…not sure…what to say," Dave responded haltingly.

"If I may be a little forward, I'd like to repeat that she is the one who missed out! I'm glad she can't see what a wonderful person you are. Heck, you saved her life. You're a hero. You are a knight in shining armor. What girl doesn't dream of that? Apparently, Stephanie missed that story. I don't want to sound like I don't like her, or am envious of her, I just want you to hear what I think of her missed opportunity."

April was pouring it on, and Dave's ego was burgeoning. Even if she was being a little malicious toward Stephanie, it didn't bother Dave as much as he thought it might. Maybe it was because April was boosting his non-existent ego, or maybe he was just open for any ideas on how to get Stephanie out of his mind.

In the world of campus gossip, Dave had heard some remark that "April can be a little demanding." Others even went so far as to describe her as a "control freak." These comments came from reliable sources that not only knew Dave, but also had been in class with April. They may have been a little strong in their description of her, but Dave didn't seem to mind. Becoming the school gossip for the past few months put Dave on the school radar. Some called him a hero. Some called him an idiot for thinking he had a chance with Stephanie just because he saved her life.

Being treated by April as if he were some sort of knight in shining armor was nice. Still, Dave was naturally cautious about flattery. Was she up to something? His suspicious mind wasn't sure if this was just a game that April was playing. Then when the temporary stardom wears off, will April, Stephanie, or any of the girls around campus give him the time of day?

After several hours of talking to April on the phone, Dave said his goodbyes and went to bed. His dreams were filled with scenarios involving April. His subconscious was playing havoc with this new relationship.

On one hand, Dave thought he was in love with Stephanie. On the other hand, no matter how he tried to suppress it, he was falling for April. He wondered if all guys go through these kinds of emotions. Could it just be hormones, or could it be blind love?

CHAPTER 19

Several weeks passed, during which a nonstop text and phone call marathon was played out. April and Dave became inseparable. Dave's antisocial behavior was dissipating rapidly. It was as if he had become an extrovert overnight. Students at school were saying "hey" when he walked by, and girls were eyeing him. He almost went through all of high school in obscurity. Now during his last quarter, he has become almost popular. He felt good, and he felt happy that April was paying attention to him.

Dave and April's nights were spent talking endlessly on the phone about nothing. School days were spent with the two trying to catch up between classes occasionally getting to class late. Dave drove April home after school every day, or to work when she didn't have dance class. On weekends, when neither had to work, they spent their time at the beach. It was a life to be envied. Dave was happier than a pig in slop.

The relationship was solid until the afternoon when Dave was invited to a party out at Eric Kray's house. Dave rarely (actually *never*) went to parties in the past. However, Dave's flowering social life seemed to require him to do things that he previously had considered beyond him or immature. Eric and he had grown up together all through school from kindergarten. They never really associated much out of school, but were in the same classes throughout their school years.

Eric lived out east in the country with his mom. His dad was never around, which made it easy for him to develop a free spirit. That also made it easy for Eric to do whatever he pleased. In his mother's hopeless attempt to gain her son's respect, she bought the booze for his parties. His mom was a hard working single woman trying to give Eric a good life. He loved her very much, but always seemed to have disagreements about the direction he was heading. Eric was well liked in school, so Dave's association with him made it easier for him to move among the inner circles now that he was becoming more social.

No one knows for sure why Dave decided to go to Eric's party. He knew that April wouldn't go because there was going to be drinking. Nevertheless, he invited her to go with him. He tried to convince her that it was one of the last parties of the year before everyone would go their own way. In an attempt to be more popular, Dave ignored his natural instinct for avoiding what he used to consider such a shallow event. He felt that it wouldn't hurt to ride the popularity wagon to the end.

Dave was correct. April refused to go to the party. In no uncertain terms, she spelled out for Dave why he should not go either. In fact, April could hardly believe Dave's decision. The indignation in her tone with Dave was apparent. He knew he would have to pay for his decision, but he felt this was a decision he was going to make without April's intervention.

The party was in full swing by the time Dave arrived. Eric's mom was there with several of her friends. Eric and James were arguing about paintball, and the rest were dancing, smoking, or drinking themselves into a stupor. They had two kegerators set up, and several beer bongs.

Eric's mom introduced Dave to one of her girlfriends. Her name was Daisy. She had enough tattoos on her to start a picture book, and sported some 'classy' leathers. She was a biker chic from Rubonia Heights. She was no stranger to these underage drinking parties.

After an hour or so of mingling, Dave ended up on the porch swing with Daisy. He found out that she was thirty-seven years old and had two kids. Her kids were living with her ex-husband and his wife, and that she worked the afternoon shift at Wally World.

Over a number of beers, and a shot or three of Jack Daniels whiskey, Dave unfolded his story about Stephanie, and now April. Daisy sat there barely conscious listening intently to him. After he finished, he looked into her eyes for some confirmation, affirmation, or insight of any kind.

Daisy looked back at Dave in silence before saying "Excuse me for just one second."

She got up from the swing as quickly as she could, stumbled the two steps to the railing of the porch, grabbed the railing with both hands, bent over almost in half, and vomited her insides out for what seemed like more than five minutes. Dave became very nauseous.

Still hurling, Daisy let loose a fart that was almost inhuman in its proportions. She slowly turned to sit back down on the swing wiping the excess sputum from her mouth with her arm, and said, "Excuse me."

The front of her top was cluttered with bits and pieces of vomit. She either didn't notice it, or didn't think it mattered that it was still there. She made no attempt to brush it off.

After sitting back on the swing, Daisy pulled at her shorts, which were stuck in her behind, readjusted her bra, picked some debris out of her hair, and wiped her arm on her shirt, before she made the following observation:

"You know, Dave, it seems to me that you had no chance with the Stephanie girl because of her social status and her taste for much taller guys. That may be why you thought you were in love with her. Men always want what they can't have. And, with that April girl, you were looking for a pretty skirt with a big shoulder to cry on. In fact, from what you have said she is even higher on the food chain. I believe that you suffer from the upgrade syndrome, and don't have the wherewithal to step it up. Now, I want you to take me for an example. I'm a simple woman who doesn't expect much from a man. Yeah, I do hope that he has a job, and a valid driver's license. Truth be told, even that doesn't usually stop me from hanging out with a guy. Do you see where I going with this, Dave?"

Dave looked at her as well as he could with one eye open. The alcohol was making its rounds through his system wave after wave, so he may have missed a word or two. In his polluted mind, he tried to analyze what she was trying to say. On one hand she thought Stephanie was a girl running a bit on the wild side who was too good for him, and on the other hand she was certain that April was nowhere in any league he could play in. This revelation sent him into a deep depression. Dave went silent, becoming sullen.

Daisy continued her analysis.

"And another thing, Dave. Take a guy like you. Yeah, you're nice, but girls don't always want a nice guy. Whenever I have a nice guy hitting on me, I just give him the evil eye and show him my gold teeth. That usually gets rid of him. You need to be a little rough once in a while."

Dave sat there in amazement while Daisy continued to lecture him on his biggest fault: being too nice. He didn't have a chance to land a "real woman." He didn't have a hope of ever attracting a girl of good breeding. Somehow, Daisy convinced him that the only chance he had in life was to settle for a girl like her. *She* didn't expect much. *She* didn't demand much. Above all, *she* was a biker chic with a cigarette flopping about in her mouth. What more could he ask for?

He knew something was askew with her revelation, but the drink had clouded his mind like the marine layer over the Golden Gate Bridge. The next thing he knew he was on the back of Daisy's bike heading away from the party.

He woke up to a Sunday morning in a confused state of mind. The sun was peaking in the bedroom window through the dusty old rags, in lieu of curtains. A cigarette was burning in the ashtray next to the bed, and you could see rays of sun catching the smoke trails as they ascended into oblivion. This certainly was not home. *Where in hell am I*, Dave screamed inside, while holding his aching head.

He lifted up what appeared to be a sheet draped over him and noticed that he was not only naked, but he had a few scratch marks on his body that he was sure he didn't have the day before. He was laying on a strange bed with a stained, thin, almost white sheet drawn across his body, and no fitted sheet or mattress pad that he could see. Dave shuttered as he observed the top sheet. It looked like it had been used to catch oil leaks from under a motorcycle. In fact, a Harley was parked right there next to the bed. Piles of dirty clothes were strewn around this poor excuse for a bedroom. Where was he? His throbbing brain began to rifle through the confused memories of the previous night hoping for an explanation.

Before he could figure anything out Daisy walked into the bedroom with an old TV tray filled with odds and ends of what appeared to be former table scraps. It looked like she had carefully placed month old leftovers, and two vile smelling cups of coffee on the tray. Daisy stood there in her birthday suit and biker boots. Reality hit Dave like a ton of bricks. Had he spent the night with this wrinkled, saggy, multi stomached, tattooed woman with droopy knees? Worse, he may have done something, for the first time with a woman, who was old enough to be his mother, and he didn't even remember doing it!

It was too much to bear. He slumped back and closed his eyes. What have I done? Did I really spend the night with this woman? Did we really do it? Dave punished himself with thoughts of things he may have done.

"I gotcha breakfast here, darlin'. We can have breakfast in bed just like they do in the movies. After a while I'll show you 'round my place, but for now let's eat something so you can get your strength back. You'll need your strength for a repeat."

"What do you mean, repeat?"

"Repeat of last night! I ain't had a man handle me like that for a long time. You…"

"Okay, I get it. I have a headache. Can we not talk about last night?"

With as much dignity as Dave could muster, he offered a few lame excuses for not staying for breakfast. He dressed as quickly as possible, and walked out of the house, closing the sliding glass door behind him. Now outside, it took Dave several minutes to realize that his truck wasn't there. He stood looking up to the sky wondering if God was watching.

Daisy appeared in the doorway with a smile. Dave turned to face his impending doom. She had thrown on some *very* short shorts, a white tank top without a bra, and a worn do rag. Rounding out this nightmarish ensemble, a cigarette dangled from her bottom lip and gator skin biker boots hung from her hairy unshaven legs. Without a word, she saddled up on her Harley, pushed it out the sliding glass door, and waited for Dave to close the door and hop on the back of the bike.

She took him back to Eric's house to get his truck. Luckily, there wasn't anyone awake to see them pull up. It had been one of those nights that one might say was "motivated by the booze." Dave was definitely going to use *that* excuse to explain his actions especially if anyone ever found out he spent the night with Daisy. He didn't ask Daisy what happened. He just got off the bike and headed for his truck. "What a fool," he kept saying over and over in his head.

Monday came sooner than Dave wanted it to. He wasn't sure who knew what about that night at the party. He only hoped that his obscurity at school would stay intact. After second period, April caught up with him near her geometry class. Dave was playing it cool hoping she would not be too inquisitive.

"Hey, Dave. How was the party?"

"It was okay. They did have drinking going on like you thought they would. I have to admit I did have a couple drinks." Dave cringed. He thought for sure that April would pitch a fit, but she dropped the subject. Instead, she asked Dave if he wanted to take her to Adventure Island that coming weekend. She had a season pass, and her mom gave her a one-day pass from the time she went up. The only expense would be for the gasoline. Dave stumbled over his words, but eventually said yes.

He wondered whether he had gotten away with it. If word of his '*excursion*' with Daisy were to become public knowledge, certainly April would have dumped him by now. High school gossip travels faster than the speed of light. Surely if someone had seen him ride off with Daisy someone would have said so. Maybe no one really cared whether he went with her or not.

"Sure. Let's go on Saturday."

"Gotta go!" April chirped.

"Me too," Dave responded with a fake smile. If he didn't know anything, Dave knew that Daisy was not a case of blind love, but a mistake of circumstance.

CHAPTER 20

Adventure Island makes for a peculiar date. You go to the park, and eat, then ride, then eat, then ride. Conversation with any depth doesn't happen in an amusement park. The whole time is spent screaming or mumbling; about how hot you are, how tired you are, how bored you are from standing in line. The same talking points come up in every queue. Where are you from? What's up with the weather? You ask countless strangers where they live or go to school and then pretend to know where that place is. The useless, just-to-pass-the-time tidbits that come up in line are simply astounding.

The drive home was long. Dave and April spoke no more than a couple of words because April slept most of the way home. Dave nodded off once or twice, only for a split second. Even during these brief flashes of semi-consciousness, his mind began to contemplate the relationship he *could have had* with Stephanie. If only she loved him a fraction of how much he loved her. April was a different matter. Dave was not sure where *that* relationship was going. His hopes were for eternal bliss, but reality had a way of interfering with his dreams. Would the Daisy guilt haunt him for the rest of his life? Would he ever go back and ask what happened that night?

When he reviewed the recent past, it was clear, that in the beginning, it looked like God had put Stephanie right into his arms. What an illusion that turned out to be. Then, after almost getting over the disappointment of Stephanie, Dave took up with April. Her infatuation with him was a welcome change of pace, but if he really cared about April why did he go to that party? He wondered if she felt the same as he did about her. Would it last? Would they survive if she found out about Daisy?

It was probably a week before Eric mentioned anything to Dave about the party. They were hanging out at the Big L drinking sweet tea. Dave and Eric were parked side by side in the Big L parking lot watching cars go by. When Dave jumped out of his truck to go in and get a sweet tea refill Eric spouted out as Dave walked past his truck, "Did you have a good time with Daisy?"

Dave stopped in his tracks, turned, and walked back the two steps to Eric's side of the truck. He looked both ways as if to be on the lookout for anyone who might be listening in or the conversation..

"What are you talking about?" Dave answered.

"My mom told me the story that Daisy told her."

Eric began to laugh and grab his stomach, nearly swallowing his chew. It was obvious that Dave's little mishap was out, and the chance of it staying behind closed doors was not going to happen. Although Dave could already figure out what was coming next, he only hoped he would be able to keep Eric from opening his mouth around everyone else. Dave contained his anger, and tried to change the subject; thinking it might make the experience disappear.

"I thought I might go pick up a bracelet or some earrings for April." Dave commented. Eric was still holding back, choking on his chew when Dave finished.

"What? Are you thinking? Do you think that a piece of jewelry will buy April off if she hears about your outing with Daisy?"

Eric spit out what chew he hadn't already swallowed from the laughing. He looked intently at Dave's serious face, and said,

"You have got to be kidding. When she finds out what you did there is no amount of jewelry you can buy that will keep her at your door. I really don't like to say this, but you are done for."

"Maybe if I..."

"Forget it Dave. You are all washed up with that girl. Those kinds of girls can order up on any menu they choose, but guys like us only get the scraps. You were shopping in the wrong store when you thought you could impress Stephanie, and you are still in the wrong store with April. Just give up and face the fact that your chances with that kind of real estate is hopeless."

"I know. I don't want to seem desperate, but why can't I at least give it a shot?"

"You can. That's all guys like us can do. We don't have a chance when it comes to getting high-class girls like April or Stephanie. Those Ivy League guys always end up with them."

Dave contemplated the conversation as he walked in to the restaurant to get a refill of sweet tea. He was in trouble with no way out. He may have lost his love over a few shots of Jack Daniels. Things like this are not suppose to happen when you are in love, or do they? Maybe that is why it's called blind love.

CHAPTER 21

Dave was sleeping when the phone rang. It was Sunday, two o'clock in the morning.

"Dave. Are you asleep?"

"Ahh, ahh, no. I was just.... Is that you Stephanie?"

"Yeah. Could you come after me?"

"Ahh, sure. Where are you?"

"I'm at Matt Casey's house at a party. Do you know where he lives?"

"He lives in the green house just off Erie road doesn't he?"

"Yeah. That's it. You'll see a bunch of cars out front. You can't miss it."

"Is everything all right? You aren't hurt or anything are you?"

"No. I'll tell you all about it when you pick me up. I want to get out of here."

"Okay. I'll be there shortly."

Was he dreaming? Dave contemplated this mystery as he stumbled to the door with his keys in one hand, and his right shoe in the other. He wasn't going to waste any time getting over there to rescue Stephanie. His damsel was in distress. With his shining armor almost on, he hopped in his truck and sped out of the drive to save the day.

Stephanie was standing out front near the mailbox when Dave pulled up. She quickly got into his truck, looked directly at him, and said, "Let's get out of here. Now." Dave was confused as to where she wanted to go, but, from the look on her face, he wasn't going to ask her where. Stephanie had tears streaming down her cheeks. She was grasping her cardigan with clenched fists. It was clear that she was not happy with someone. Dave continued driving slowly in the dark, hoping she would come out of her shell for a moment and tell him where she wanted him to take her.

It may have been a minute. It may have been ten minutes. Whatever the case, Stephanie finally wiped away the tears, sniffled a little, took a gasp of air, and began pouring her heart out to Dave. From what Dave could decipher between the sniffles and sobs, Stephanie and Jake had broken up again. She caught him at the party making out with Jessica Lovejoy. Jake's 'love' for Stephanie was obviously not enough to keep him from "*getting some*" from another girl.

Jake had made a feeble attempt to make a couple stereotypical excuses like, "It didn't mean anything," and "I didn't know what I was doing because I was drinking too much." The lame justifications didn't hold any water this time. It was very hard for Stephanie to believe anything he was saying while he was standing there with his pants down in the laundry room while Jessica sat on the dryer quietly pulling up her panties.

Finally, Stephanie provided Dave with some direction. "Let's go down to the marina park."

"Okay," Dave agreed.

Taking a right on Second Street, after coming into town, he parked under a light at the park. His mind began to race as it had before with all kinds of thoughts; none of which were making much sense. One thing was clear, and that was that he was in deep trouble. The Daisy incident is all but out. When April finds out about it, she will not accept any excuse however well contrived. When she discovers that he picked Stephanie up at a party, after she had been drinking, the rescue excuses will evaporate quickly. All Dave could do was to sit there and contemplate the loneliness that is soon to come upon him.

To make things worse Stephanie slid over next to Dave, and laid her head on his shoulder. He stiffened up, taking a breath and tightening up his muscles. It seems, to be a guy thing. Whenever guys get close to a girl, or even see a cute girl, they seem to want to suck in their stomach and puff up their chest. It must be a male mating ritual. As Stephanie closed her tear filled eyes and fell asleep in a whimper, Dave contemplated his life again. The love of his life was within his grasp, but the thought of April continued to haunt him. Does this mean he might have a chance to move in on Stephanie? If so, then he won't care if April finds out about Daisy. Contemplation wore him out and soon even with all of the drama Dave fell asleep.

The bright morning sun and the noise of the traffic woke Dave. Stephanie was sleeping with her head in his lap curled up in a ball on the seat. Dave had a stiff neck from leaning against the truck window all night. People were stirring. Couples and small groups of people were passing by on the sidewalk going for their morning walk. The sea gulls and pelicans were busy swooping and diving, and an old man with a furry kind of dog stopped just in front of Dave's truck so the dog could urinate on the light pole.

As Dave wiped the sleep from his eyes, he could only wonder what this new day would hold. If only he could have controlled himself, he wouldn't be considering alternatives. Could he quit drinking? Was drinking his coping mechanism? The second-guessing went on for some time as he went through all of the stupid choices he had made, and missed opportunities that were lost forever.

Stephanie woke up with a headache, and mumbled something about her disheveled appearance. She finally looked at Dave after one additional adjustment and said, "This doesn't constitute sleeping together does it?"

"What?" Dave exclaimed.

"Well. I don't want you to get the wrong idea about me. I was in trouble again, and you saved me from a messy situation, again. I wouldn't want anyone to think that I called you to bail me out of a sticky situation…in order to sleep with me."

"Stephanie, you know that I would do anything for you, anytime. I'm not going to start any bad rumors. I'm not even going to entertain thoughts of spending the night with you… well maybe in my dreams, but… Anyway, I have a stiff neck from leaning against the truck window all night, and my leg is asleep. As for your love life, I've never seemed to be on your radar. So, what happened last night at that party is really none of my business. Of course I wish you and I could be more than friends. I would never treat you the way you have been treated. I think you have already realized that I care very much for you."

"You know you are the only guy I have ever known that thought of me as a person—not just a piece of…well, you know. I can't talk to those jocks about stuff like you and I can. Even though I was in a coma I could occasionally hear your voice as you read or talked to me. It's not that I don't like you— I do, but my life is so complicated right now. You understand don't you?"

Dave turned toward Stephanie, beaming with appreciation. "That makes me feel real good when you talk that way. You see, Stephanie, I'm really looking for a strong relationship that is not solely based on sex. I want a girlfriend, and eventually a wife who I can call my best friend. I want to be with someone who is thinking *'bout growing old together*. I want to be with someone who cares about what my interests are as much as I do hers. I know, this sounds corny, and all grown up, but it is the truth. I could only *dream* that you were that person. I know you are not oblivious to my feelings toward you. Even if it can never happen, you can be assured that I will always be there for you. I realize that I'll never be good enough for you."

"Please don't say that, Dave. You saved my life. You've been there for me. Don't think I can't see that. I guess I'm prone to gravitate toward the jocks. I know there may be some jocks that want a true relationship likc you described, but I'm doubtful there are many. Plus, it must be my fate, or a comfort zone for me to be going out with jocks."

Dave pursed his lip nervously. "You may know that I am going out with April now. We have been seeing each other some. I won't tell you that it isn't somewhat serious, but that's because I never thought I had a chance with you. It just happened. Actually, I have been saying that too much lately. I apparently have a need for more excuses than I can tolerate these days."

"Whatever are you talking about Dave?"

"Never mind Stephanie. I was just talking to myself about my life as of late."

"What is April going to say about that thing with that biker chic? You know she is not the kind of girl that could understand that kind of action. She doesn't drink or party, so she would not have any idea what you went through."

"You know about that too? Oh, God! My life is surely over. April's innocence is what draws me to her. I know if I had another chance, I could change, but the way it looks she will surely find out about Daisy and dump me. I know I deserve it."

"Guys don't change, Dave. Oh, they say they will change in order to convince a girl to do what they want. Then they go back to the way they were. They *return to their own vomit* like it says in the Bible."

Dave leaned towards Stephanie, confidently. "Well, I'm going to be one of the ones who *will* change. If I weather this Daisy ordeal with April, I promise myself that I will change no matter what. I *will* quit drinking, going to party's where there is booze and drugs, and start going to church. I know I can change."

Dave paused, grabbed the back of his neck as if to assure himself that he had enough backbone, and then continued. "If I did change in this way would it help your interest in me? You know I would do whatever it took to get you to love me."

"You can't get someone to love you, Dave. They either love you or not. Sure, it helps when you act sincere. You know that girls are emotional about flowers and jewelry, but there's more to it than that. And, when you do shower them with gifts they naturally think you want repayment for expenses rendered. Guys don't mind the investment as long as the return is going to be worth it."

"Not *all* guys are that way," Dave insisted.

Stephanie looked away for a moment. Turning back to Dave, her voice lowered, "I have to go. Would you please take me home? I want to get a shower and get ready to go shopping with my mom."

Dave dropped Stephanie off at home, and headed back to the farm. His obvious love for Stephanie was still intact. All the way home he contemplated what the reasons might be that she didn't find him attractive enough, muscular enough, tall enough, or something. She's prone to gravitate toward guys who are much taller, but being vertically challenged didn't seem to be something that she would hold against a guy; would she?

How is it possible to be torn between two loves? Dave's head was in a spin. He had to revive his ambition to change, especially if April found out about the Daisy incident. And, from what it looked like, Stephanie was not likely to change her ways any time soon. Dave concluded that the best he could do was to try to carry on and pray that April would never find out about Daisy. He realized that high school love is blind.

BLIND LOVE   AARON ELKIN

To this day, Dave still puzzles over the nature of a man's first encounter with blind love, and how it affects the rest of a person's life.

As a teen it is hard to understand that seemingly insignificant decisions could become crucial elements of one's future. Without the benefit of hindsight, it is difficult to comprehend that *choices* are unsolved *opportunities* that need to be addressed with a clear head. Last but not least, without wisdom it is unlikely that a young man or woman will see excuses for what they are: the result of poor choices.

THE END

Printed in the United States
152951LV00001B/15/P